The Adventures of Spider-Man

Adapted by Michael Teitelbaum

Based on the screenplay by David Koepp

Photography by Zade Rosenthal and Peter Stone

AVON BOOKS

An Imprint of HarperCollinsPublishers

COLUMBIA PICTURES PRESENTS A MARVEL ENTERPRISES PRODUCTION A LAURA ZISKIN PRODUCTION "SPIDER-MAN"
STARRING: TOBEY MAGUIRE WILLEM DAFOE KIRSTEN DUNST JAMES FRANCO CLIFF ROBERTSON ROSEMARY HARRIS
MUSIC BY DANNY ELFMAN EXECUTIVE PRODUCERS AVI ARAD STAN LEE SCREENPLAY BY DAVID KOEPP BASED ON THE MARVEL COMIC BOOK BY STAN LEE PRODUCED BY LAURA ZISKIN IAN BRYCE DIRECTED BY SAM RAIMI

MARVEL

sony.com/Spider-Man

COLUMBIA
PICTURES

Library of Congress Catalog Card Number: 2001118008
ISBN 0-06-441073-0

First Avon edition, 2002

AVON TRADEMARK REG. U.S. PAT. OFF. AND IN OTHER COUNTRIES,
MARCA REGISTRADA, HECHO EN U.S.A.

❖

Visit us on the World Wide Web!
www.harperchildrens.com
GO FOR THE ULTIMATE SPIN AT
www.sony.com/Spider-Man

To Stan Lee and Steve Ditko for their brilliant creation;
To Mike Hobson and John Romita for the magazine;
And to my mom and dad, who—back when you could
buy two comic books and piece of gum for 25 cents—
always gave me that quarter.

PROLOGUE

Who am I, you ask? Are you sure you want to know? You say you want hear the story of my life. That story is not for the faint of heart.

If somebody said that my story was a happy little tale, if somebody told you I was just your average, ordinary guy without a care in the world . . .

. . . then somebody lied.

Mine is the story of a boy whose parents died when he was four years old. It's the tale of a scared, lonely, and confused child grasping the hand of a social worker as if it meant his very life, then releasing that grasp to go live with an aunt and uncle he hardly knew.

It's the story of a lonely childhood spent with books and chemistry sets, rather than other kids, as best friends.

Yes, mine is a tale of pain and sorrow, loss and grief, longing and heartache, anger and betrayal. And that just covers the high-school years.

My story, like so many worth telling, is also about a boy and a girl. About true feelings kept bottled up for years, about a lonely, shy boy desperate to tell the girl how he felt, yet so terrified of rejection, that he kept his those feelings hidden until he felt he might explode.

The girl? Her name is Mary Jane Watson. M.J. to her friends. She's the woman I've loved since before I even knew I liked girls.

The boy? I'm sure you've guessed. The boy is me.

Who am I? Well, you did ask. I go by the name . . . Spider-Man!

CHAPTER 1

The ancient yellow school bus rattled along the pothole-riddled streets of Queens, New York. Looking as if it had been in service since before its passengers were born, the bus contained thirty high-school students.

Inside, the usual morning pandemonium was well underway. Laughing, yelling, joking, yawning, singing, and a few unidentifiable grunts and groans filled the bus as it rumbled through the streets.

"Mmm," moaned one student as he sank his teeth into a greasy jelly doughnut, a stream of red glop and a cloud of powdered sugar landing on his pants.

Another student drummed on his notebook with two pencils, eyes closed, head bobbing in rhythm to the music pouring from his headphones.

"Hey, spaz, where's my homework?" came a shout from the back.

"I'm doing it now!" came the strained, high-pitched reply.

A handsome, muscular boy sat with his arm around the shoulder of a pretty, red-haired girl. He glanced out the window and spotted someone running alongside the bus, desperately trying to catch up to it.

"Hey, look!" the athletic boy shouted. "Parker missed the bus again! Or maybe he's just trying out for the track team!"

Everyone on the bus exploded into derisive laughter. Everyone except the red-haired girl, who lifted the large, beefy arm from her shoulder and got up from her seat. She looked out the window and sighed deeply.

"Stop the bus!" she shouted, to be heard over the laughter. "He's been chasing us since Woodhaven Boulevard!"

Outside, seventeen-year-old Peter Parker ran as fast as his skinny legs would carry him. He was late for the bus, as usual, and had been running after it for seven blocks. Sweat flew from his forehead as he struggled to keep his legs pumping, his arms around his books, and his glasses on the slippery bridge of his nose.

The bus slowed to a stop and the doors creaked open. Peter eased his run to a trot, then a walk. Breathing heavily, he stumbled up the stairs, limping from the pain in his calf.

"Sorry, I'm sorry," he said, making his way down the aisle, bumping into feet and knocking over backpacks. Peter spied an empty seat next to a girl. Their eyes met for a moment.

"Don't even think about sitting here, geek," the girl muttered, grabbing her books and plopping them down on the vacant seat.

Peter continued, shuffling awkwardly down the aisle, fumbling with his books and shoving his glasses back up his nose with his index finger. Too busy looking for a seat,

Peter didn't notice the large foot now sticking out into the aisle.

"Oomph!" Peter groaned, as he tripped and went down hard, slamming into the floor, face first, his books scattering everywhere.

"Flash Thompson!" the red-haired girl shouted at the handsome, muscular boy in the seat beside her. "Why did you do that?'

"Do what?" Flash replied, shrugging innocently.

"Oh, give me a break, Flash," the girl said, getting to her feet. "I know you stuck your foot out to trip Peter."

"Come on, Mary Jane," Flash pleaded. "Would I do something like that?"

Mary Jane stepped past Flash into the aisle and started picking up Peter's books. Peter, still stunned, looked up at her with his glasses dangling from one ear, and smiled.

CHAPTER 2

This was no ordinary day for the students in Peter's class. They were not headed toward their high school, but rather for a field trip to prestigious Columbia University in Manhattan.

Turning onto the Queensboro Bridge, the school bus left the neighborhoods of Queens behind. Ahead, the gleaming skyline of Manhattan came into view, rising from the island like the Emerald City in the land of Oz.

Peter felt the familiar rush of excitement that always accompanied a trip into "the city," as those in the outer boroughs called Manhattan. And for him, like so many of his classmates, the lure of Manhattan was both thrilling and terrifying. Peter would be graduating soon and giving a lot of thought to the idea of moving into Manhattan to begin his life after high school.

As the bus turned onto upper Broadway, the austere spires of Columbia University came into view. Its gated campus provided a refuge from the nonstop energy of life in Manhattan, and its Ivy League students were among the brightest in the nation.

Wow! was all Peter could think as he caught his first glimpse of the beautiful stone buildings. In addition to living and working in Manhattan, Peter also had dreams of going to college, though at the moment, despite his good grades, the idea of attending Columbia University seemed like an impossible dream.

The bus squealed to a stop. Its door opened and out poured the high school students, still restless and exuberant with the morning's unspent energy. For weeks Peter had been looking forward to the lecture/demonstration they were about to attend. After all, it was a science demonstration, and science was by far his favorite subject.

Peter's science teacher, Mr. Hecht, came bounding up the stone steps in front of the Columbia University Genetic Research Institute. He quickly raced to the top step of the building so he could keep an eye on his rambunctious students.

"Okay, people, no wandering!" he shouted over the din of yelling and kidding around and conversation. "Proceed directly up to the—*hey!* Knock it off, people! Listen up! Can we please pretend that we are young ladies and gentlemen here, at least for one day? Proceed up the stairs and into the building. That means you, Thompson!"

One of Flash Thompson's buddies punched him playfully on the arm, then thought better of the move when Flash returned the blow, not so playfully. One or two students started slowly up the steps. Most of the others continued to stand around, talking.

A chauffer-driven car slowly pulled up to the curb near Peter. In the back sat a father and son.

"Dad, could you drive around the corner?" the son

asked, embarrassment showing on his face.

"Why, Harry?" the father asked sternly. "The door's right here."

"These are public school kids, Dad," Harry replied, slumping down in the seat. "I'm not showing up to school in a Bentley!"

"What?" Harry's father barked angrily. "You want me to trade my Bentley for a Volkswagen because you flunked out of every private school I sent you to?"

"They were not for me!" Harry snapped back. "I told you that. It wasn't me."

"Of course it was!" Harry's father shouted, reaching past his son and opening Harry's door. "Don't ever be ashamed of who you are. Remember that."

"Dad," Harry began, sighing deeply. "I'm not ashamed. I'm just not what you—"

"What, Harry?" his father interrupted.

"Forget it, Dad," Harry moaned, slipping out of the car, closing the door behind him. He turned around and found himself face to face with Peter.

"Hiya, Harry," Peter said, flashing his friend a big grin. Peter's camera hung around his neck. He was hoping to get some good shots of the demonstrations they were about to see.

"Hey, Peter," Harry replied, dejectedly.

The back door of the Bentley flew open, and the intimidating figure of Harry's father stepped from the car. "Won't you be needing this?" he said, handing Harry his backpack.

Harry nodded. "Peter," he began. "This is my father, Norman Osborn."

"It's a great honor to meet you," Peter said, extending his hand. Norman grasped the hand and shook it firmly.

Out of the corner of his eye, Harry noticed Mary Jane and a few of her girlfriends pointing at the Bentley and whispering.

"I've heard a lot about you, Peter," Norman Osborn announced. "Harry tells me you're quite the science whiz."

"Well, I don't know about that," Peter said, shrugging.

"He's being modest," Harry chimed in, his focus now back on his father and Peter. "I told you, Dad, Peter's won all the science fair prizes."

"Well, anyone who can get Harry to pass chemistry shouldn't be modest," Norman said, glaring at his son.

"Harry's really smart, Mr. Osborn," Peter said quickly, sensing the tension between them. "He didn't really need my help."

Harry glanced up the stairs and saw the last few of his classmates entering the building. "We have to go, Dad," he said, trying to bring the conversation to an end.

His father ignored the cue. "I'm something of a scientist myself, Peter," Norman announced, his imposing presence seeming to grow with the boast.

"Oh, I know," Peter replied quickly. "I know all about OsCorp. You guys are designing the guidance and reentry systems for the first shuttle mission to Mars. The stuff your company works on is really brilliant."

"Impressive," Norman said, a tight-lipped grin turning up the corners of his mouth. "Your parents must be proud."

"I live with my aunt and uncle," Peter explained, returning the smile. "And yes, they're proud, thanks."

"What about your folks?" Norman asked, his face turning serious.

"My parents died when I was little," Peter replied.

Norman sighed deeply and nodded his head. "I also lost my parents as a young boy," he said.

"Which no doubt strengthened your famous iron will to succeed, huh, Dad?" Harry chimed in, unable to disguise his annoyance. "Look, we really have to—"

"Hey, you two!" Mr. Hecht boomed, sticking his head out the door. "I'm closing the door, now!"

Peter started backing up the steps. "Nice to meet you, Mr. Osborn," he said, turning and heading toward the door, followed closely by Harry.

"I'm sure I'll see you again, Peter," Norman called out. Then he slipped back into his car without even a glance at Harry.

Peter stepped into the Research Institute, excited about the demonstration he was about to see. Little did he know that by the time he left this ornate, impressive building, his life would never again be the same.

CHAPTER 3

The main lobby of the Columbia University Genetic Research Institute was a cavernous marble circle. Tall fluted columns rose to a brilliant white ceiling, and hallways led off the circle like spokes on a wagon wheel.

Despite his continued protests, Mr. Hecht couldn't keep the noise level down, as the high-school students milled about the lobby, waiting for further instructions.

"Your dad doesn't seem so bad," Peter said as he and Harry joined their classmates.

"Not if you're a genius," Harry replied with a smirk. "I think he wants to adopt you." Harry nudged Peter gently and tilted his head toward a group of students huddled around one of the lobby's columns.

Peter glanced at the group and spotted Mary Jane. His eyes opened wide and he swallowed hard. He had been crazy about M.J. ever since she moved next door to him when they were both in elementary school. Peter would have loved nothing more than to date his pretty, popular, outgoing neighbor, but he had not yet worked up the courage to ask her out.

Harry started walking toward her. Peter followed.

"Hey," Harry said casually as they joined the group. "How you doing?"

"Hey," Mary Jane replied.

"Say something," Harry whispered to Peter. "Here's your chance."

Mary Jane smiled at Peter. He returned the smile, but said nothing. The moment passed. Peter walked away, with Harry right behind him.

"Why didn't you say anything?" Harry asked Peter, when they were back across the lobby.

"I was about to," Peter replied defensively. "It just wasn't the right moment."

"Well, what are you waiting for?" Harry asked, shaking his head. "An engraved invitation?"

"All right, people," Mr. Hecht shouted. "They're ready for us. Now, I want adult behavior. Is that clear?"

For the first time all day, his students were quiet.

"Let's go," the teacher continued, heading down one of the many the hallways leading from the lobby. "Follow me."

The class gathered inside a large laboratory. The footsteps of the thirty students, their teacher, and a tour guide echoed in the huge room, bouncing off the high arching ceiling and the hard marble floors. Various displays were scattered around the lab, but they all had a common theme—spiders.

"There are more than thirty-two thousand known species of spider in the world," the tour guide began, his deep voice filling the room. "All spiders are carnivorous, ravenous eaters who feed on massive quantities of protein in liquid form, usually the juices of their prey. Spiders, of course, are not insects. They belong to a group of small animals called arachnids. Other arachnids include scorpions and mites."

Peter's interest drifted from the tour guide's lecture over to Mary Jane and her friends. He couldn't help staring at her as she and her group, which included Flash Thompson, giggled, joked around, and generally showed no interest in the lecture.

As Peter watched, Flash put his arm around M.J. and leaned his face in close to hers. Peter winced and turned away, a move that did not go unnoticed by Mary Jane. Embarrassed, she pulled away from Flash and pretended to pay attention to the tour guide.

"Different types of spiders possess varying degrees of strength, which helps them in their constant search for food," the guide continued. He pointed to a glass case in which a large brown spider stood motionless in its web. "For example, the jumping spider, genus *Salticus*—"

"Excuse me!" Mr. Hecht shouted at his class, noticing a lack of interest on the part of a number of his students. "Is anyone paying attention to the genus *Salticus*?" He turned to the tour guide. "I apologize. Go on."

The guide continued. "The genus *Salticus* can leap distances up to forty times its body length, thanks to a proportionate muscular strength vastly greater than that of a human being."

Peter caught the eye of the tour guide and pointed to his camera. "Is it okay if I shoot a couple of pictures for the school paper?" he asked.

The tour guide nodded and went on with his lecture. As the guide spoke, Peter lined up a shot of the spider in the glass case. Just as he snapped the photograph, one of Flash's buddies muttered "Geek!" and bumped Peter's arm, ruining the picture.

"Hey!" Peter grumbled, looking at Justin, who stared at the tour guide, flashing a smile of mock innocence.

"The funnel web spider, genus *Atrax*, is one of the deadliest spiders in the world," the guide continued. "It spins an intricate, funnel-shaped web whose strands have a tensile strength proportionately equal to the type of high-tension wire used in bridge building."

Peter raised his camera again, lined up another shot, and again Flash's buddy bumped his arm. Peter turned and glared at the boy. So did Harry.

"Leave him alone," Harry muttered tersely.

"Or what?" the boy asked defiantly, a look of contempt on his face.

"Or his father will fire your father!" Flash replied quickly.

Those in earshot of the exchange giggled.

"That's it!" Mr. Hecht shouted, startling both his students and the tour guide. "The next person who talks is going to fail this course." Whispers and giggles broke out among the students.

"I kid you not!" Mr. Hecht blustered. He nodded for the tour guide to continue.

"The crab spider, genus *Misumena*, hunts its prey using a set of amazingly fast reflexes. Its nerve impulses move with such astonishing speed that some researchers believe it almost borders on precognition. In other words, it seems to know when danger is going to strike before it happens. Call it a 'spider sense,' if you will."

The tour group moved to the center of the lab where a team of researchers sat at computer keyboards. The computers were all connected to an electron microscope, which in turn was tied into a series of large video screens all around the room. Each screen contained the unmistakable image of DNA strands—spider DNA.

"Over five painstaking years, Columbia's genetic research facility has fully mapped the genetic code of each of the three types of spiders I have just discussed," the guide explained. "Using these DNA blueprints, we have now begun what was once thought to be impossible—inter-species genetic blending."

The class gathered around a large glass tank in the center of the lab. Inside the tank, strange-looking spiders crawled and spun webbing.

Mary Jane's eyes opened wide as she stared at the creeping creatures. She smiled and said, "Disgusting!"

Harry was standing beside her. "Hateful little things," he said. He would have said anything to agree with her. Although he knew of Peter's feelings toward M.J., Harry also found the vivacious redhead extremely attractive.

"No," Mary Jane whispered. "I think they're cool."

Not sure whether she was serious or not, Harry played it safe. "Really?" he said. "Me too."

The lecture continued. "In our lab, we have combined genetic information from these three types of spiders. The resulting spiders each have the strength and jumping ability of the jumping spider, the incredibly strong webbing of the funnel web spider, and the spider sense of the crab spider. In short, we have created these fifteen genetically designed super-spiders, the first mankind has ever produced."

For the first time, the class' full attention was focused on the specimens before it, and on the tour guide's words.

He went on, the excitement unmistakable in his voice. "Just imagine, if one day we can isolate the strengths, powers, and immunities in human beings, and transfer that DNA code among ourselves, all disease could be wiped out. Of course, we're nowhere near ready to start experimenting with humans, so for the moment we're concentrating on these fifteen mutant spiders. Any questions?"

"Aren't there only fourteen spiders in there?" M.J. asked, pointing to the tank.

"No," the guide replied. "There are fifteen. I think."

In a curved arch of the lab's ceiling, high above the marble floor, a mutant spider scurried across the thin strand of its powerful webbing. Unnoticed by the crowd below, the genetically designed spider left the center of its web and began its descent to the lab's floor.

As the tour continued, Mary Jane stopped at a glass display tank and checked out her reflection, pushing a few copper-colored strands of hair away from her eyes.

"Mind if I take your picture?" asked a voice from behind her.

Startled, she turned and saw Peter, his camera raised to his eye.

"I need a shot with a student in it," he explained.

"Okay," M.J. agreed. "Just don't make me ugly!"

"Impossible!" Peter replied, focusing his lens. "Right there. Hold it. Great!"

As Peter snapped the shot, the mutant spider dropped

with increasing speed. It was now only several feet above Peter's head.

"One more, M.J.," Peter said, taking another photo. "Thanks." Mary Jane turned and ran off to join her friends.

The mutant spider leaped from its thin strand of web, landing on the back of Peter's right hand.

"Ow!" Peter yelped as the spider's fangs pierced his skin.

CHAPTER 4

Peter stumbled backward in shock, shaking his hand. He snapped his wrist back, sending the spider flying. Clutching his throbbing right hand with his left, he stared down at two tiny red marks just below his right knuckles. Images from vampire movies flashed through his mind as he glanced at the dead spider on the floor beside him.

A warm, sickening numbness spread up Peter's right arm, as the throbbing in his hand continued. The lights in the lab grew dim. Glancing around, he discovered that the rest of his class had already moved on. He was alone, confused, and frightened. *Home,* he thought. *Must get home!*

Somewhere through the pain, fear, and strange sensation which started in his arm and now washed over his whole body, came the thought *They'll never miss me. No one will even notice I'm gone!*

Peter staggered from the lab, back through the lobby, and out into the bright Manhattan afternoon. His face was pale and sweat poured from his forehead. He thought of taking the subway home, but wondered if he could stay conscious long enough to be awake for his stop. At that moment, his classmates came pouring through the door to the Institute and raced passed him, down the long steps.

"Hey, what's the matter, Parker?" Flash Thompson taunted him. "Did those eensy-weensy spiders scare you?"

"Are you all right, Peter?" Mary Jane asked, noticing his sickly complexion and dazed look.

"Huh?" Peter mumbled. "Yeah, I'm okay."

"What's the matter with you?" Harry asked, stepping up beside Peter. "You look like you've just seen a ghost."

"I don't know," Peter lied. "I guess I'm coming down with the flu or something."

Peter joined his classmates on the bus for the trip back to Queens. He sat alone in the back, sleeping for most of the trip. Restless dreams featuring giant spiders filled his uneasy slumber. When the bus finally reached his stop, the driver had to shake Peter to rouse him from his deep sleep.

The modest house in the quiet Queens neighborhood that May and Ben Parker called home looked pretty much like all the other houses on the block. A green shingled roof sloped down to meet the red brick exterior. Small front yards planted with hedges and flowers were surrounded by gated chain-link fences.

As evening fell, dogs barked, children played stickball in the street, and the working-class people who were longtime residents made their way home from work.

Inside the Parker home, Ben balanced himself on a chair, his hands extended above his head in an attempt to reach the lightbulb he hoped to change. Ben Parker was a tall man in his late sixties. He kept himself in good shape, staying trim and active. His kind face was crowned by a thick shock of white hair.

"Why don't you use a ladder, Ben?" May Parker asked, shaking her head. The same age as her husband, May Parker appeared thin and frail, though her spirit was youthful and strong. "Better yet, just wait for Peter to come home. He can do that."

May and Ben Parker had been as true a mother and father to their nephew as any child ever had. They loved Peter like a son, and he shared that affection many times over.

Ben screwed in the new bulb and light flooded the kitchen. "You were saying?" Ben commented, looking down at May with a look of triumph.

"Great," May replied, sighing. Ben was a stubborn man. It frustrated May sometimes, but it was also one of the things she loved about him. "Now get down before you end up on your butt!"

"I'm already on my butt!" Ben exclaimed, stepping off the chair. "When the plant's senior electrician is laid off after thirty-five years, that's what I call being on your butt!"

While May prepared dinner, Ben sat at the kitchen table flipping through the want ads in the paper. "You'll get another job, Ben," she said confidently. "Somewhere."

"Let's see," Ben said, running his finger down the column of job listings. "Computer analyst, computer designer, computer engineer." He slammed his fist on the table. "I'm sixty-eight years old! How am I supposed to provide for my family in today's world!"

May put down the bowl she was holding and hugged her husband. "I love you," she said, gently kissing Ben on the check. "And Peter loves you. You're the most responsible man I've ever known. We've been down before, but somehow we survive." She glanced up at the clock. "Where is Peter, anyway? He's late."

As if on cue, the front door swung open and Peter stepped into the house, trying his best not to give away his condition.

"Here he is," Ben said, closing the paper so Peter wouldn't see him looking at the want ads. "How was the field trip, Peter?"

"You're just in time for dinner, dear," May announced.

Peter reached the stairs, clutching the banister for support. "Don't feel well," he mumbled. "I'm heading up to go to sleep."

"You won't have a bite?" May asked.

Peter turned sharply toward his aunt, the image of the mutant spider flashing through his mind. Then he realized her meaning. "No thanks," he replied, stumbling up the steps. "Had a bite already."

"Did you get any good pictures, Peter?" Ben asked.

"No," Peter muttered. "I mean, yeah. I mean, I've got to go crash. Need some sleep. Don't worry, everything's fine." Then he scrambled up the remaining stairs and disappeared into his room, slamming the door behind him. "Now what was that all about?" Ben asked, rising from the table.

"He's a teenager," May replied, following Ben.

"He's depressed," Ben said, starting up the stairs. He thought of all the times Peter had come home from elementary school crying because none of the other kids would play with him. Ben was still very tuned in to his sensitive nephew's moods. "I better go up and talk to him."

"He's a teenager," May repeated, putting her hand on Ben's shoulder. "Stay put. He'll let us know if he needs help."

In his bedroom, Peter dropped to his knees, clutching his stomach in pain. The warm, numb feeling that had spread throughout his body had now changed to terrible chills, like those that came with a high fever. He was dizzy and nauseous and felt as if he was going to faint. But this was no flu.

Examining the back of his right hand, Peter saw that the spider bite was now red and swollen. Drenched in sweat, he trembled violently, teeth chattering. His face turned white and his sunken eyes rolled back into his head. Then his eyelids closed and Peter passed out, slumping to the carpet next to his bed.

Just before he lost consciousness he mumbled a single word. "Help . . ."

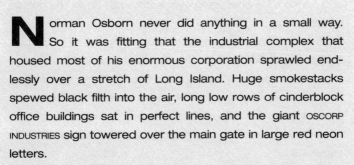

CHAPTER 5

Norman Osborn never did anything in a small way. So it was fitting that the industrial complex that housed most of his enormous corporation sprawled endlessly over a stretch of Long Island. Huge smokestacks spewed black filth into the air, long low rows of cinderblock office buildings sat in perfect lines, and the giant OSCORP INDUSTRIES sign towered over the main gate in large red neon letters.

Deep in an underground laboratory, almost directly below this sign, Norman Osborn stepped briskly down a hallway. His nervous assistant Ms. Simkins followed, struggling to keep up with Osborn's rapid pace. They stepped through a pair of doors that slid open automatically, and proceeded into the sprawling main lab of the research-and-development section of OsCorp.

"General Slocum and the others from the Pentagon have already started the inspection," Ms. Simkins said anxiously. "Mr. Balkan and Mr. Fargas are with them."

"Why wasn't I told about this, Simkins?" Osborn said fiercely under his breath.

"I don't think they wanted you to know, sir," she replied sheepishly.

Osborn and Simkins approached a group of visitors in the center of the lab. Some were dressed in military uniforms, some in business suits, and others in white lab coats.

They were all huddled around a strange-looking object mounted on a pole. Technicians fiddled with the object, which looked like a large Boogie board or snowboard with wings on either side. Footholds were carved into each wing, and a long tube containing a jet engine ran down the middle of the board.

One technician wore a tight-fitting suit. Wires and electronic relays ran through the suit like veins behind human skin. When the technician moved his right arm, the winged board leaned to the right. When he lowered his head, the board's front tilted down. The device responded instantly to his every move, but the visitors didn't seem particularly impressed.

Standing next to the odd-looking contraption, Dr. Mendel Stromm, the project director, prepared to address the group. Stromm was a brilliant scientist and the man Norman Osborn had always depended on to keep his company at the cutting edge of technology. The combination of Stromm's scientific genius and Osborn's bulldog tenacity had turned OsCorp into one of the most successful corporations in the world. But both men were very aware of just how fragile that success could be.

"Our work on the Individual Personnel Transport is moving along splendidly," Stromm announced to his guests.

"I've seen your little glider, here," replied General Slocum, the leader of the visiting group. Slocum was all army, from the medals on his uniform to the military haircut, to his no-nonsense attitude. "That's not why I'm here."

"Ah, General Slocum," Norman Osborn said as he and Simkins joined the group. "Good to see you again." Osborn quickly made eye contact with the others who had gathered. "Mr. Balkan, Mr. Fargas. Always a pleasure to have our board of directors visit."

Balkan and Fargas were both in their late seventies. Fargas was confined to a wheelchair. Both men looked displeased at Osborn's arrival.

"I want a progress report on your Human Performance Enhancers," General Slocum blurted out, bored with the corporate niceties.

Stromm stepped forward, pointing to a glass isolation chamber across the room. Inside the chamber, a team of scientists made adjustments to a complex-looking bank of equipment.

"We tried vapor inhalation with rodent subjects," Stromm explained. "They showed an eight-hundred percent increase in strength."

"Eight-hundred percent?" Fargas asked, rolling his wheelchair closer to Stromm and Slocum. "That's excellent!"

"Any side effects?" asked the general.

"In one trial, yes," Stromm began. "The rats—"

Osborn quickly cut him off. "It was an aberration," he said. "A minor, one-time thing. All the tests since then have been successful."

General Slocum ignored Osborn and spoke directly to Dr. Stromm. "In the test that went wrong, what happened?"

the general asked. "What were the side effects?"

"Violence, aggression, and, eventually, insanity," Stromm replied, avoiding eye contact with his boss.

"What's your recommendation, Dr. Stromm?" General Slocum asked.

Osborn jumped in before Stromm could speak. "With the exception of Dr. Stromm, our entire staff has certified that the product is ready for human testing," Osborn said proudly. "We are ready to create an enhanced human being."

"I disagree," Stromm stated firmly. "I believe we need to start from scratch, redesigning the formula."

"Redesign the formula!" Osborn shouted, seething with rage.

For the first time General Slocum turned and stared at Osborn. "Mr. Osborn, you have missed seven consecutive delivery dates," he began. "After five and a half years of research and development, the United States government has a right to expect the super-soldier you were hired to deliver."

"These are quantum leaps in science you're asking for, General," Osborn explained, his even-toned voice and cool exterior hiding the tightening in his stomach. "We are unlocking the secrets of human evolution. I never said it would be cheap or fast, only that it would be groundbreaking."

"Let me make this nice and simple for you, Mr. Osborn," General Slocum said, placing his hat on his head, a clear signal that this meeting was about to end. "If your so-called Human Performance Enhancers haven't had a successful test on a human in two weeks' time, I will pull your funding and give it to Quest Aerospace."

Osborn winced at the mention of his greatest competitor.

The two members of OsCorp's board of directors moved closer to Norman. "The general has given the go-ahead to Quest to build their own version of a super-soldier," Mr. Balkan explained. "I would hate to see our funding go to them. Wouldn't you, Norman?"

"Yes, Norman," added Mr. Fargas, glaring up at Osborn from his wheelchair. "I think we would all hate to lose this funding. Now, the question is, Norman, what are you going to do about it?"

CHAPTER 6

Golden early-morning sunlight poured into Peter Parker's bedroom. Peter lay sprawled on the floor in the same exact position he had collapsed into the night before. Slowly he began to stir.

He pulled his arms up from his sides and lifted his face off the carpet. Swinging his legs around and pulling himself into a seated position, Peter's head started to clear. Taking a deep breath, he remembered the bizarre events of the day before. And then he realized something—he felt better! Much better!

Bounding to his feet, Peter had the strange sensation that he, in fact, felt better than he ever had in his whole life. He slipped his glasses on and everything went fuzzy. *Huh?* he thought. *Usually I can't see a thing without my glasses.* Whipping them off, everything became crystal clear. He tried them again. On, fuzzy; off, clear.

"Weird," he muttered.

Leaving his glasses off, Peter caught a glimpse of his clock. *Oh, no! Late again! Gotta hustle!* He pulled off the T-shirt he had slept in, then gasped at what he saw in the mirror.

There stood Peter Parker, who had never been near a

weight room in his life, with a perfect physique—clearly defined pecs, washboard abs, bulging biceps. It was as if someone had placed his head on the body of a guy who worked out every day.

"Wow!" he yelled. "What is going on!"

A knock came at his bedroom door. "Peter?" Aunt May called. "Are you all right?"

"Fine, Aunt May!" he called back. "I'm fine. Never better!"

"Any change from yesterday?" Aunt May asked.

"Oh, yeah," Peter replied, tossing his glasses into the garbage can. "A big change!"

Peter dressed in a hurry, bounded down the stairs, and leaped over the banister, landing like an Olympic gymnast right behind Uncle Ben.

"Morning," he said, stuffing an English muffin into his mouth. "Late. Gotta go."

"We thought you were sick," Uncle Ben said.

"I was," Peter replied, grabbing food with both hands from whatever plate he could reach. "I got better."

"Sit down, dear," Aunt May pleaded.

"Can't," Peter answered, kissing his aunt on the cheek. "See you later."

"Don't forget," Uncle Ben said. "You're helping me paint the kitchen right after school today, remember?"

"Sure thing, Uncle Ben," Peter said, smiling, grabbing more food. "Don't start without me."

He dashed through the front door, checking his watch, hoping he was in time to catch Mary Jane.

"Now what in the world was that about?" Aunt May asked when the door closed behind Peter.

"I don't know," Uncle Ben grumbled. "But he just ate my bacon!"

Peter stepped outside just in time to see Mary Jane leave her house. She paused outside her front door as a voice boomed from inside her house.

"I don't care what your mother said," shouted the harsh, slurred voice. "You're trash. You'll always be trash. Just like her."

Mary Jane looked back at her father for a moment. "I have to go to school," she said, turning and walking away quickly.

"Who's stopping you?" Mr. Watson yelled back.

"Leave her alone," said a weak voice from inside the house.

"Who's talking to you?" Mr. Watson screamed at his wife. Then he slammed the door shut.

Mary Jane rushed across the street, fighting unsuccessfully to hold back her tears. A scene like this one was not unusual for the Watson household. But the fact that it happened often didn't make it any easier to deal with.

Peter walked on the opposite sidewalk, keeping pace with M.J. but staying far enough back so that she didn't see him. "Talk to her," he muttered to himself, trying to build up his confidence. "Just talk to her." Then he noticed her tears. *No*, he thought. *It'll just embarrass her to know that I caught that touching little family moment.*

A car horn startled both Peter and M.J., as a convertible driven by Flash Thompson pulled up beside Mary Jane. The car was full of her friends, and she quickly wiped away her tears and pasted a big, happy smile on her face.

"Thanks for the ride," she said, hopping in.

As the car sped off, Peter caught the sound of M.J.'s carefree laughter rising above the roar of the engine.

Peter approached the bus stop, only to see the school bus pull away. "Not again," he cried, then broke into a sprint. Amazingly, within seconds he had easily caught up to the bus—and he wasn't even out of breath.

Reaching out to pound on the bus, hoping to get the driver to stop, Peter's hand caught a school banner which was attached to the side of the bus. The banner said, GO WILDCATS!, the name used by Midtown High's athletic teams.

As Peter touched the banner, the bus picked up speed and pulled away—but the banner stuck to the palm of his hand, tearing loose from the accelerating vehicle. *What is going on?* Peter wondered for the fourth or fifth time that morning, as he pried the banner loose.

The deafening blast of a truck horn shocked Peter. He turned and saw the grill of a huge semi only inches from his nose.

Yaaaiii! Peter shrieked, moving instinctively.

Screeeechh! The driver slammed on his brakes, knowing full well that he did not have enough time to stop before slamming into the boy in the street. When the truck lurched to a halt the driver frantically scrambled out of the cab. Racing to the front of his vehicle, he looked at the grill. Nothing on it. Then he looked down on the ground. No one there. Pulling off his baseball cap and scratching his head, he climbed back into the truck and drove away.

Peter slowly opened his eyes. He glanced down and saw the street—ten stories below! Looking up, he realized that he was near the roof of a tall apartment building, sticking to a brick wall by the palms of his hands and the bottoms of his feet.

I jumped up here, he thought. *That's the only explanation. I jumped up here, and now I'm sticking to the side of the building!*

Peter reached out and grabbed a thick metal drainpipe which ran down the length of the building. Hoping to pull himself up onto the roof, he squeezed the pipe with one hand—and crushed it like a piece of aluminum foil. Loosening his grip, Peter plunged toward the sidewalk, where he landed on his feet, unhurt.

Exhilarated, terrified, and still in shock, Peter ran down the street toward his school.

CHAPTER 7

The cafeteria at Midtown High School was a bustling scene of lunchtime mayhem. Students gathered around long tables, laughing and chatting. Others waited in line for the day's special to be plopped onto plates and tossed onto their trays. Occasionally food would fly through the air, landing on a table, the floor, or a student.

Peter Parker, still pondering the great change that had come over him, made his way through the maze of tables, carrying enough food on his tray to feed ten people. In addition to the physical changes and the strange new abilities that were part of his transformation, Peter was hungry. Very hungry. All the time. Easing into a chair at one of the few uncrowded tables, Peter began to shovel meatloaf and mashed potatoes into his mouth.

Mary Jane strolled past, on the way to a table filled with her friends. Her tray blocked her view of the floor, and so she didn't see the pile of gravy-ladened potatoes as she stepped on it. Her feet slipped out from under her, the tray went sailing into the air.

Peter saw that M.J. was going to hit the floor hard. Moving

instinctively, he leaped from his chair, grabbing M.J.'s flying tray with his left hand then reaching down with his right arm, catching her around the waist just before she hit the ground.

M.J. regained her balance and Peter handed her the tray. "Wow!" she said. "Great reflexes! Thanks!"

Peter shrugged. He couldn't believe he had just pulled off the acrobatic maneuver, either. It felt to him as if his very thought had instantly translated into movement. "No problem," he said calmly.

"Hey," Mary Jane said, pointing at Peter's face. "You have blue eyes. I guess I never saw you without your glasses. Did you just get contacts?"

"Uh," Peter stammered, certainly not ready to discuss what he was going through, as he wasn't sure about it himself. "Uh-huh."

M.J. smiled, waiting for Peter to continue their conversation.

He said nothing.

"Well, se ya," M.J. finally said, turning away.

Peter clenched his jaw. Another missed opportunity.

Just before she reached her table, M.J. turned back and smiled at Peter. Then she sat down next to Flash Thompson.

Peter took his seat and resumed his meal, going through two main portions and four desserts before pausing to take a sip of his milk. He put his fork down, but when he lifted his hand to grab the milk carton, the fork stuck to his fingers.

Puzzled, Peter once again yanked on the fork to pull it free. A long gooey strand running from the fork to his right wrist stretched like a strand of melted cheese on a slice of pizza. Only this strand was stickier and stronger. Peter could not remove the fork. Lifting his left hand to try to free the fork, a long strand shot from his left wrist and caught the tray of a girl sitting at the next table.

Peter pulled hard with his left hand, finally freeing the fork from his right. The motion caused the long strand from his left wrist to snap the tray away from the girl and send it flying right at Peter's head.

He ducked and the tray sailed over his head—only to come crashing down, right on Flash Thompson.

Flash spun around, enraged. "Parker!" he shouted. "Have you lost your mind?"

As Mary Jane try to hide her laughter from Flash, Peter ran from the cafeteria.

Alone in the hallway, Peter looked down at his wrists and noticed a tiny slit in each one. *These were definitely not there yesterday!* he thought as he rolled his sleeves down and buttoned them to conceal his wrists.

That's when the strangest sensation he'd ever had washed over Peter. Time seemed to slow down, and everyone around him appeared to move in slow motion. He also felt as if he could see what was going on around him, in all directions at once, as if his vision had expanded to cover three hundred and sixty degrees.

He saw a fist heading for the back of his head. Time suddenly returned to normal as Peter spun around and stepped to the side—just in time to avoid a powerful punch from Flash Thompson.

Flash's beefy fist missed Peter's head and slammed into a locker with a loud clang.

"Ow!" Flash cried, shaking his hand. Then he stared at

Peter, seething. "You think you're pretty funny, don't you, freak!"

Mary Jane stepped between the two boys. "Flash, it was an accident!" she said.

"I'm sorry," Peter quickly added. "It really was."

"No," Flash snarled. "My fist breaking your teeth, that's an accident!"

"I don't want to fight you, Flash," Peter said, as a crowd began to form.

"I wouldn't want to fight me, either," Flash replied, as Mary Jane stepped aside, realizing there was nothing she could do to stop this.

Flash threw two quick punches, and Peter easily dodged them both. Flash looked stunned, not able to understand how this uncoordinated bookworm could possibly move so quickly.

One of Flash's pals tried to grab Peter from behind, but Peter sensed him coming and ducked, then stood up quickly, flipping him over his back.

"That's it, Parker!" Flash roared. "Now you're dead!" He rushed at Peter, arms flailing, punching wildly.

Peter never even moved his feet. Bending at the waist, he avoided every blow, with time to spare.

Mary Jane turned to Harry Osborn, who had joined the crowd. "Harry, please help him," she pleaded.

"Which one?" Harry replied, clearly enjoying his buddy's success in frustrating the school bully.

Flash charged at Peter, head down, and ran right into Peter's fist. The punch landed squarely on Flash's jaw and the larger boy went flying off his feet, crashing into a bank of lockers, then slumping to the floor unconscious.

"Look what you did, Parker," Flash's buddy shouted, squatting beside his battered friend. "You knocked him out."

"I didn't mean to," Peter replied, looking down at his own fist, shocked by his newfound strength.

The crowd that had gathered for the fight closed in around Flash. Normally the toughest kid in school, the fallen giant now sprawled pathetically on the floor, suddenly a figure of sympathy.

Students looked up at Peter strangely, as if he had become some kind of monster. Glancing down at his own hands, Peter was suddenly frightened of his incredible new power.

He ran from the school. *I have to find out what these powers are*, he thought, his mind racing.

CHAPTER 8

Standing in an empty alley, Peter looked back and forth from his hands to the brick wall in front of him. "Here goes nothing," he muttered.

Placing his hands on the wall, high above his head, Peter pulled himself up. His palms stuck to the bricks, as if they had suction cups attached. Reaching up with one hand, then the other, Peter scurried up the wall in seconds, landing gracefully on the building's roof.

"This is amazing!" he shouted, running at full speed, then leaping from the roof's edge. Soaring over the alleyway, he landed gently on the roof of an adjacent building, then continued his aerial journey, bounding from rooftop to rooftop.

"I've got to try something," Peter said, his heart pounding. Standing at the edge of a rooftop, he aimed his wrist at the building across the alley. Trying to remember exactly what he had done in the cafeteria to make the strand shoot from the slit in his wrist, he squeezed his hand into a fist.

Nothing happened.

He twisted his hand in all directions. Still, nothing happened. Rotating his hand so the palm faced up, he pressed his ring and middle fingers into his palm.

Thwip!

A single strand of webbing shot from his wrist, sticking to the wall across the way. Peter tugged on the webbing. It held fast. "Here goes nothing," he muttered. Then he grasped the strand tightly and stepped from the roof.

"It works!" he shouted with excitement, swinging like a monkey on a vine, the powerful strand supporting his weight. Then he looked up and saw a brick wall coming toward him rapidly.

"Whoa!" he cried. "Where are brakes on this thing?" Extending his legs in front of him, Peter slammed into the wall, feet first, then rammed it with his shoulder and finally his face.

I guess I need more practice! he thought as he dangled in a daze.

Peter spent the rest of the afternoon and evening wall-crawling, web-swinging, and leaping around neighborhood rooftops, fine-tuning his abilities.

As night fell, he finally headed home. On the way, he tried to sort out the bizarre events of the last few days. *When that mutant spider bit me, it must have somehow transferred its abilities to me. I've become some kind of human spider. Weird!*

Arriving at home, Peter stepped into the kitchen and was instantly hit by the smell of wet paint. "Oh, no," he said. "I promised Uncle Ben I'd help him paint tonight." He found a note taped to the painting ladder that read: *Dinner's in the oven. We've gone to play bridge at the Andersons'.*

"Aw, shoot!" he mumbled, hating the fact that he had let his uncle down.

Loud shouting from next door broke his train of thought. Looking out the window, he saw the silhouettes of Mary Jane and her parents. They were arguing again.

Peter stepped out into his backyard just as Mary Jane shoved her back door open and stormed out into her yard. "Oh, hi there," he said, embarrassed to be caught.

"Were you listening to that?" M.J. asked.

"No. Yeah," Peter stumbled with his words. "I mean, I guess I heard something."

"I'm sorry," M.J. said. "We do that all the time. Your aunt and uncle never scream."

"Oh, they can scream pretty good, you know," Peter replied, trying to make her feel better.

"So," M.J. began, quickly changing the subject. "What are you going to do after we graduate?"

"I thought I'd move into the city, get a job as photographer, and work my way through college," Peter explained. "What about you?"

"I guess I'm headed for the city too," M.J. replied. "To be an actress."

"Hey, that's great," Peter said. "I think great things are coming for you, Mary Jane."

"Oh, yeah?" she said. "And what's coming for you?"

"I'm not sure," Peter answered. "But it feels like something I've never felt before. Something . . . different."

An awkward moment of silence passed between them.

"You know, you're taller than you look," M.J. said, reaching out, grabbing Peter's arms. She was surprised by his bulging biceps. "Don't slouch so much."

M.J. kept her hands on Peter's arms. His heart pounded.

Then the shouting in M.J.'s house resumed and a loud car horn blared, shattering the moment.

Flash Thompson pulled into the driveway, behind the wheel of a brand-new convertible. "Hey, M.J.," Flash shouted. "Come take a ride in my birthday present!"

Mary Jane looked at Flash, then back at Peter. "Thanks, Pete," she said, shrugging. "I've got to go." She smiled at Peter, then hopped into the convertible and drove away.

Peter flexed his bicep. The muscle grew huge. He sighed and shrugged. *Big deal*, he thought.

That night, alone in his room, Peter thought about his new-found powers as he flipped through the newspaper. An ad jumped out at him.

ATTENTION AMATEUR WRESTLERS!
THREE THOUSAND DOLLARS
if you can stay in the ring for three minutes
with Bone Saw McGraw.
Colorful Characters a MUST!

"That's it," Peter cried, tearing the ad from the paper. "I can pick up some quick cash to buy a car of my own!"

Grabbing a pencil and a sketch pad, Peter got to work designing a costume for himself. Two, three, four sketches ended up crumpled on the floor before Peter took a break and decided to practice his web shooting.

Setting up a series of bottles on his bookcase, he tried to hit each one with a blast of webbing. Although he could now control *when* his webbing fired, he had no way to precisely aim the streaking strands. Each shot missed by a large margin, slamming into the bookcase, knocking books and science fair awards to the floor.

"Peter!" Aunt May called from down the hall. "What's going on in there?"

"Just exercising, Aunt May!" Peter shouted.

"Well don't hurt yourself, for goodness sake," she replied.

Peter pulled out his tools and began rummaging through his drawers for anything he thought might help him create a device to improve the aim of his web shooting. He spread old toys, watches, and other junk across the top of his desk. Firing up his soldering iron, he got to work.

Just another science project for Peter, he thought, smiling, as he cobbled together a pair of web-shooting wrist bracelets. Slipping them onto his wrists, he fired at the first bottle on his shelf.

Thwip! A direct hit! He yanked his arm back and the bottle went flying across the room, smashing into a wall.

"Hey!" Uncle Ben shouted from downstairs. "What are you doing up there?"

"Studying, Uncle Ben!" Peter called out. "Studying really hard!"

CHAPTER 9

Even in the dead of night, the tall smokestacks of OsCorp's industrial complex belched black fumes into the air.

In the research and development lab deep underground, all the scientists, technicians, and other OsCorp employees had gone home. All except for Norman Osborn and Dr. Mendel Stromm.

Osborn stood in a glass-walled isolation chamber in the center of the lab. The chamber pulsed and glowed with throbbing green light as Osborn prepared himself for an experiment.

"Mr. Osborn, please don't do this," Stromm pleaded with his boss. "I'm asking you for the last time."

"Don't be a coward, Stromm," Osborn shot back. "Risks are part of laboratory science. Always have been."

"Let me reschedule this with a proper medical staff and a volunteer," Stromm suggested. "If you just give me two weeks—"

"Stromm, in two weeks this project, this company, will be dead!" Osborn shouted. "You heard the general. If we can't prove that our Human Performance Enhancers work, our funding will go to Quest Aerospace, and that'll be the end of OsCorp. I'm going to prove they work—on me! Who better to become the first human to tap into man's physical and intellectual potential? My strength and intellect will grow to super-human proportions. Then they'll see I was right!"

Stromm sighed and shook his head. He knew better than to argue with his boss once he had made up his mind. Norman Osborn was going ahead with this experiment, no matter what the cost.

"Begin," Osborn said.

Stromm flipped switches and adjusted levels on the control panel before him. Inside the glass chamber a loud hum built in intensity. Osborn closed his eyes tightly, as a thick white gas filled the chamber.

Holding his breath, Osborn felt the heavy fumes enter his nostrils. Calming himself, he exhaled, then inhaled deeply, the foul-smelling gas filling his lungs.

A burning sensation spread across his chest, but as Osborn kept breathing in and out smoothly, a sense of well-being flooded his body and mind.

That's when the spasms started.

Osborn's entire body began to shake and twitch, his teeth chattering, his arms and legs quaking violently.

On the monitor, which Stromm watched carefully, all of Osborn's life signs—heart rate, breathing, blood pressure—plunged dangerously. Stromm panicked. He knew what these readings meant. In a few seconds his boss would be dead.

Stromm slammed a large red button with the palm of his

hand. Instantly, an emergency vacuum system sucked the white gas from Osborn's chamber. Stromm yanked open the door to the chamber, rushed in, and ripped open Osborn's shirt.

Pressing his ear to Osborn's chest, Stromm heard nothing. Was he too late? He was about to perform CPR when the monitors on his control panel rang out with warning alarms. Osborn's life signs returned, then continued to rise to dangerously high levels.

Stromm was still looking back at his control panel when Osborn's eyelids shot open wide, his eyes darting left and right. He roared like an animal.

"Mr. Osborn, please," Stromm began, turning to face his boss. He never finished.

Osborn slammed his arm into Stromm's chest, sending the scientist smashing through the wall of the glass chamber, which exploded into a million tiny fragments.

Stromm sailed across the lab, slamming into a support pillar and crumbling to the floor in a lifeless heap.

Norman Osborn stepped from the shattered chamber, not as the person he had been when he entered it, but as something different, something new and strange, no longer fully human. He staggered across the room and looked down at Stromm's dead body, which sat in a pool of blood.

Then something caught his eye. He stumbled over to the high-tech glider and control suit that stood in the center of the lab. Norman Osborn tossed his head back and howled, an unnatural, inhuman shriek of pain and confusion.

Of transformation.

* * *

Norman Osborn's apartment was a study in power and style. Though the furniture was modern, the lavish apartment was decorated with ancient artifacts from many cultures, collected during his lifetime of world travels. This collection was dominated by a series of tribal masks, all based on the same theme—warfare. Norman Osborn took his business, and everything else in his life, very seriously.

On the morning after the experiment, Norman sat on the couch in his den wearing the same clothes he had worn the night before. He stared at the wall in a daze, his mind cloudy, his body aching.

Harry Osborn rushed toward the front door on his way out to school, hoisting his backpack onto his shoulders. He glanced into the den and stopped short.

"Dad, are you okay?" he asked, moving to his father's side. "You look sick. What happened?"

"I honestly don't know," Norman replied.

"Where were you last night?" Harry asked kneeling down, looking his father in the eyes. "I didn't hear you come in."

"I was . . . last night I was," Norman stammered. "I really don't remember."

Loud voices sounded from down the hallway. "I have to see him," stated one voice firmly.

Harry recognized the voice. It was Ms. Simkins, his father's assistant.

"He can't be disturbed now," said the other voice, which Harry knew to be that of his father's housekeeper.

Ms. Simkins entered the den anyway.

"Who's there?" Norman called, squinting at the intruder.

"I'm sorry, Mr. Osborn," Ms. Simkins said, walking toward Norman.

Harry stepped in front of Simkins. "My father is not well, Ms. Simkins," he explained.

She stepped around Harry and knelt next to Norman. "Mr. Osborn," she began. "Dr. Stromm is dead."

"What?" Norman exclaimed, jumping to his feet.

"His body was found this morning in the laboratory," Ms. Simkins reported. "It appears that he was murdered."

"What are you talking about?" Norman demanded through the fog inside his head.

"Also, sir," she continued. "The flying wing glider prototype is missing. It's been stolen."

Norman straightened up, fighting to clear his thinking. "Take me there," he said firmly. "Now."

CHAPTER 10

Peter bolted down the stairs heading for the front door, his book bag slapping against his side. "Going to the library, see you later, bye!" He blurted the words out so fast they sounded like one long word.

"Hold on!" Uncle Ben called out, grabbing his jacket and car keys. "I'll drive you."

"It's okay," Peter replied quickly. "I'll take the train."

"I said I'll drive you," Uncle Ben said sternly. "Get in the car."

Peter knew better than to argue with his uncle when he used that tone of voice. The two slipped into Uncle Ben's Oldsmobile. After a quiet ride, Uncle Ben pulled his car to the curb in front of the Forty-Second Street public library.

"Thanks for the ride," Peter said, reaching for the door handle.

"Hold on a minute," Uncle Ben said firmly. "We need to talk."

"No time for a lecture, Uncle Ben." Peter moaned. "I really have to go."

Uncle Ben ignored the protest and continued. "Something has changed, Peter. Your aunt May and I don't know who you are anymore. I wonder if you even know who you are. Our Peter, starting fights in school?"

"I didn't start that fight," Peter whined, rolling his eyes.

"Something is happening to you," Uncle Ben stated flatly. "You're changing."

"How would you know?" Peter asked, unable to hide his annoyance at what felt like an interrogation.

"Because when I was your age, I went through the exact same thing," Uncle Ben answered, standing his ground.

"I don't think so," Peter shot back. "Not exactly. Look, I really have to go."

"These are the years when a man becomes the man he's going to be for the rest of his life," Uncle Ben continued, undaunted. "Just be careful who it is you change into. Like any boy becoming a young man, you're feeling this great power. But remember, with great power comes great responsibility."

"What are you afraid I'll do, become a criminal?" Peter yelled, as his uncle's meaning became clear. He almost never raised his voice to his uncle or aunt, and he wasn't sure if the anger he was feeling now was a result of the transformation he'd undergone, or just what any other teenager would feel in his situation. "Stop worrying about me, okay? Something's different! I'll figure it out. Just stop lecturing me!"

Peter shoved the car door open and stepped out.

"I know I'm not your father, Peter," Uncle Ben said through the open window, keeping his voice calm.

"Then stop pretending to be," Peter snapped back. The moment the words left his lips, he regretted saying them.

"I'll pick you up here at ten," Uncle Ben said softly. Then he pulled away from the curb.

"I'm sorry!" Peter shouted after the retreating car, wishing he could take the moment back.

Wallowing in frustration and beating himself up for speaking so harshly to the man who had raised him, Peter waited until the car vanished from his view. He turned and walked briskly from the library.

A few blocks away, Peter came to a large sports arena. A huge crowd had gathered outside and was pushing its way toward the entrance. The spotlit marquee read: WRESTLING TONIGHT! Peter pulled the crumpled newspaper ad from his pocket and unfolded it. Taking a deep breath, he joined the throng of spectators and would-be wrestlers inching their way toward the door.

Once inside, Peter made his way to a table next to a sign that read, THREE MINUTES FOR $3,000. Waiting in line behind men twice his size, dressed in all manner of strange costumes, Peter eventually signed up to wrestle Bone Saw McGraw.

Stepping into the main arena, he was overwhelmed by the noise of the cheering crowd and the brilliant spotlights sweeping across the building. In the ring, Bone Saw McGraw held his latest victim high over his head. Peter headed for the backstage area.

The massive wrestler was an amazing physical specimen. Close to seven feet tall, his body looked as if it had been chiseled from marble, every huge muscle perfectly defined. He wore no shirt, the better to expose his chest and arms. His skin-tight pants outlined his powerful leg muscles.

Bone Saw benchpressed his helpless opponent several times, his muscles rippling with the movement. The crowd leaped to its feet and roared its approval, sensing that the end was near.

"No one can last for three minutes with Bone Saw!" the monstrous grappler bellowed. Then he casually tossed his opponent over the ropes, out of the ring, and onto the floor. The nearly unconscious man landed at the feet of the fans in the front row. "Next!" Bone Saw snarled, raising his fists in triumph.

The ring announcer stood in front of a curtain on a ramp leading up to the ring. "Are you ready for more?" he shouted into a microphone.

"More! More! More!" the crowd chanted, whipped into a frenzy.

"Bone Saw is ready!" the giant in the ring yelled, stalking around, waving his arms, urging the crowd on.

"Will the next victim please enter the ring at this time!" the announcer shouted. "If he can withstand just three minutes in the ring with Bone Saw McGraw, the sum of three thousand dollars will be paid to . . ."

The announcer turned to the curtain behind him. "The Human Spider?" he whispered, his hand covering the microphone. "That's it? That's the best you got?"

Behind the curtain Peter waited anxiously. He had put on a makeshift costume made from old sweatpants and a sweatshirt, and a hood covering his head, neck, and shoulders. "The Human Spider," he said. "That's my name."

"Nah," the announcer replied, as the crowd grew impatient. "You have to jazz it up a little." Turning back to the microphone, he continued, "The sum of three thousand dollars will be paid to the terrifying, the deadly, the *amazing Spider-Man!*"

"That's The Human Spider," Peter corrected the announcer as he brushed past him.

"Get into the ring, dipstick," the announcer shot back.

Peter slipped through the ropes and took in the scene before him. Here was a student who got nervous reading an assignment in front of a class of thirty people. He now looked up at the thousands of frenzied, wild-eyed spectators, most of whom had paid for the privilege of watching him get crushed.

A noise from above brought Peter's attention back to the ring. As he looked up in horror, a huge, bottomless steel cage dropped into the ring, creating a prison for the two wrestlers. Four stagehands wrapped thick metal chains around the corners of the cage, locking the two combatants inside.

Peter grabbed the bars of the cage and shook them. They barely budged. He spun around and saw Bone Saw glaring at him from the center of the ring.

"You're going nowhere," the massive wrestler announced. "I've got you for three minutes. Three minutes of playtime with Bone Saw."

Peter swallowed hard. "What am I doing here?" he muttered under his breath.

The bell signaling the start of the match clanged loudly. Bone Saw wasted no time. The mountain of muscle charged right at Peter, who leaped straight up, leaving Bone Saw to crash into the steel bars of the cage.

Bone Saw looked up and saw Peter clinging to the top of the cage. "What do think you're doing?" he asked in shock.

"Staying away from you for three minutes," Peter explained calmly, as if he had just casually been asked for the correct time.

Bone Saw leaped up in a rage, grabbing for Peter's leg, but he moved too quickly, somersaulting across the cage, landing on the opposite side.

The crowd roared. "Go, Spider-Man!" came the cry from all sides.

"Go, Spider-Man"? Peter thought. *A moment ago they wanted to see me ground into sausage. Now it's "Go Spider-Man"?* He shrugged, deciding to give the crowd a show. Moving with blinding speed, he launched himself into a one-handed handstand—right on top of Bonesaw's head.

"Not a bad costume," Peter quipped, his confidence growing by the second. "What is that, Spandex? I tried Lycra for mine but it itched like crazy."

Bone Saw reached up and swatted Peter off his head, grabbing his ankle in the process. "I got you now, insect!" he growled, tossing Peter into the side of the cage.

"You know, technically, spiders are not insects," Peter explained as he slumped to the mat. "They belong to a group of small animals called arachnids."

Bone Saw launched himself high into the air leading with his elbows, his massive bulk headed right for Peter.

Peter flipped his feet up, catching Bone Saw in the chest, then unleashed a furious kick, sending the giant slamming into the cage's steel bars.

Bone Saw slumped to the mat, unconscious. The match

was over. The amazing Spider-Man was the winner.

The crowd went berserk, chanting "Spider-Man! Spider-Man! Spider-Man!" as flashbulbs popped and mayhem broke out in the arena.

Peter raised his arms triumphantly. "Ah, show business," he said, smiling.

Backstage, Peter waited while the promoter opened his safe and pulled out some cash. "Here's your dough," the promoter said, placing a single hundred dollar bill into Peter's palm. "Now get out of here."

"A hundred bucks?" Peter cried. "The ad said three thousand!"

"Check it again, web head," the promoter replied impatiently. "It said three grand for three minutes. You pinned him in two minutes. For that I'll give you a hundred. And you're lucky to get that. You made my best fighter look like a wimp out there."

Seething with rage, Peter grabbed the promoter by his shirt, pulling the little man close to his face. "I need that money!" he snarled threateningly.

"I missed the part where this is *my* problem," the promoter replied calmly.

It took every ounce of self-control for Peter to hold back from thrashing this man right then and there. But reason finally won out. Peter released his grip, turned, and stormed out the door—almost bumping into a short man with dyed platinum hair and beady eyes who pushed past Peter on his way into the office.

Still steaming and muttering under his breath, Peter was nearly to the elevator when he heard a shout from behind him.

"Hey! What are you doing!" came the voice. It was the promoter.

Peter spun around to see the promoter's door fling open. The platinum-haired man dashed from the office, clutching a canvas bag under his arm.

Red faced and sweating, the promoter stumbled through the doorway. "Help!" he shouted. "That guy stole all the money I made from the show! He's got my money!"

With a security guard giving chase, the thief raced toward the elevator near Peter.

"Hey, you!" the guard shouted. "Stop that guy!"

The elevator doors slid open. Peter looked at the thief racing toward the open doors, then glanced down the hall at the promoter who had just cheated him. He thought for moment, then stood by as the thief ran past him into the elevator.

"Thanks, pal," the thief snickered as the elevator doors slid shut.

"What's wrong with you!" the security guard shouted, trying to catch his breath. "You just let him go!"

The promoter ran up to Peter. "You could have taken that guy apart!" he shouted furiously. "Now he's going to get away with my money!"

Peter looked the promoter squarely in the eyes. "I missed the part where this is *my* problem," he said with a satisfied smirk. Then he turned and left the building.

Although he didn't know it at the time, it was a choice he would regret for the rest of his life.

CHAPTER 11

D ressed in street clothes, Peter walked briskly from the arena. He didn't want his uncle to know where he had really spent the evening, so he hustled, block after block, to reach the library before Uncle Ben arrived to pick him up.

At the corner where they were supposed to meet, Peter glanced at his watch. "Five after ten," he said aloud. "Hmm. It's not like Uncle Ben to be late. I hope he's not mad at me for that dumb thing I said about his not being my father. That was really a bonehead move. I've got to tell him again how sorry I am."

A police car roared past Peter, its blaring siren shattering the night. A few seconds later, an ambulance followed, siren wailing. Both vehicles made a screeching right turn onto the next block—the route Uncle Ben would be taking on the drive home.

When another police car raced by and made the same turn, a pang of fear shot through Peter's body. He walked quickly toward the next block, then broke into a jog, and finally a full-out run. Rounding the corner, his heart leaped into his throat when he spotted a huge crowd.

Shoving his way through the growing throng of onlookers, Peter emerged at the front of the crowd where three police officers stood over a body. The man's body lay sprawled in the street, blood oozing from his chest. Stepping up next to the officers, Peter looked down at the face of the dying man.

"Uncle Ben!" he shouted in disbelief, dizziness and nausea washing over him. As Peter started to kneel down next to the body, an officer grabbed his arm and yanked him away.

"Come on," the officer said. "Step aside!"

"My uncle!" Peter cried. "That's my uncle!"

The officer released his arm.

"What happened?" Peter asked, the world spinning around him in slow motion.

"Carjacker," the officer explained. "Carjacker shot him, then drove away in his car."

Peter lunged forward to reach his uncle.

"Hold on, kid," the officer shouted. "There's nothing you can do to help the guy."

"The guy?" Peter screamed, stunned that anyone could call this man who had loved him, sacrificed everything for him, "the guy."

"He's not 'the guy'!" Peter shouted back. "He's my uncle."

Peter knelt next to Uncle Ben, cradling his uncle's head in his arms. "Uncle Ben!" he called. "It's me, Peter!"

Uncle Ben's eyes opened slowly. He looked up and smiled. "Peter," he whispered weakly. Then his eyes closed and his body went limp.

Peter hugged his uncle's lifeless body close to him and cried, sobbing uncontrollably.

"They got the shooter!" a police officer behind Peter

announced, his shrill voice cutting through Peter's anguish. "He's headed south on Fifth Avenue!"

Peter's tears stopped as if someone had turned them off, anger replacing grief for the moment. Gently placing his uncle's body down onto the street, he rose, pushing his way back through the crowd, his face a mask of grim determination.

Slipping into a dark alley, Peter tore off his shirt, then ripped off his pants, revealing the costume he had worn in the wrestling ring. It wasn't much of a costume, but it would do for now.

Leaping straight up, Peter landed on the side of a building, sticking to the bricks. He scrambled swiftly to the rooftop.

Racing across the roof to the side that faced Fifth Avenue, Peter looked down and spotted a line of police cars, lights flashing, sirens screaming, all in pursuit of a single car—Uncle Ben's Oldsmobile.

Peter lifted his right hand and a gleaming strand of webbing shot from his wrist, attaching to a building across the street. Looping the webbing around his right hand, he leaped from the rooftop, swinging down in a speeding graceful arc.

The cars, lights, and people on the avenue below raced toward Peter at terrifying speed. Calmly, he extended his left hand, firing a web strand up and in front of him. As soon as the second strand had stuck to a building, he released the first one, shifting his weight to his left hand and rising once again in a sweeping curve high above the city.

Maintaining a smooth, relentless rhythm, alternating between the web shooters on each of his wrists, Peter picked up speed, web-swinging down Fifth Avenue. It only took a few minutes before he caught up to the speeding car driven by his uncle's killer.

The car swerved recklessly from lane to lane, desperately weaving through the traffic, the driver frantically trying to outrun the police cars that pursued him. Reaching an eastbound street, he cut the wheel hard, making a sharp left. The back end of the car fishtailed as he sped east toward the river. Brakes screeching and wheels squealing, the police cars followed.

So did Peter.

Thoomp!

The driver heard a dull thud on the roof, as if something had landed up there. As he looked up, puzzled, a fist smashed through the roof and a hand grasped his face tightly. Blinded, he bounced off a curb, then plowed through an intersection, cars skidding and smashing into each other to avoid him. Holding the steering wheel with one hand, the driver reached into his pocket, pulled out his gun, and fired straight up through the roof.

Blam! Blam! Blam! Blam!

Outside, clinging to the roof of the car, Peter saw the bullets explode through the shredded metal, missing him only by inches. Releasing his grip on the killer's face, he leaped onto the roof of a passing truck, which matched the Oldsmobile's speed as it rumbled along in the next lane.

Looking ahead, Peter spotted a low bridge that stretched across the street and was about to hit him, chest high. Timing his jump perfectly, he leaped off the truck, somersaulted three times as he sailed over the bridge, and landed on the truck's roof on the other side. Pausing for a moment to regain his balance, he vaulted back onto the speeding car, landing on its hood.

Ka-bash!

Peter's powerful fist smashed right through the windshield, shattering the safety glass, completely obscuring the driver's view. Careening out of control, the car crashed through the locked gates of an old warehouse right on the river, tearing the rusted ironwork from its hinges.

The car skidded toward the entrance to the warehouse, showing no sign of stopping. Seeing that he was about to be crushed against the building, Peter leaped straight up, clinging to the wall above the entrance. The Oldsmobile smashed into the warehouse, blasting the door from its frame, and jolting to a stop.

As police cars poured through the open gate, their sirens blaring and radios squawking, Peter skittered up the front of the building, disappearing through a broken window.

Inside the warehouse, Peter crawled quickly along the steel beams of the ceiling, peering down into the cavernous building. The ancient structure had been long abandoned. Rats scurried among the broken crates and rusting equipment scattered on the cement floor. The foul smell of decay mingled with the salty scent of the river, borne through empty window frames that long ago had lost their glass.

In a dark corner of the warehouse the killer looked around nervously, his gun in one hand, a canvas bag full of stolen money in the other. Police searchlights swept across the wall behind him, faintly revealing his outline. Stepping into the room to avoid being caught in the beam, he paused for a moment, looking around, expecting something, though he wasn't exactly sure what.

Slowly, silently, Peter lowered himself down from the ceiling on a single strand of webbing. The soft sound of his feet touching the dusty cement floor startled the killer, who turned and fired at the figure who had landed just behind him.

His spider sense kicking in, Peter knew the bullet was coming the instant before it left the gun. He leaped out the way, and the gunshot slammed into the wall where he had just been standing.

Blam! Blam! Blam!

Like a shooting game in some bizarre carnival midway, the killer fired at Peter again and again. With each shot, Peter leaped from wall to ceiling to floor, back to another wall, each time evading the bullet, thanks to his spider sense and amazing agility.

With blinding speed, Peter launched himself right at the killer, kicking the gun from his hand, landing in front of the man, who backed into the shadows. Grabbing the killer's shirt, Peter lifted the man off his feet.

"This is for the man you killed!" he snarled, reaching back with his right fist, unleashing a furious blow to the killer's chin, sending him flying into an unbroken window, glass raining down all around him. Peter was on him in an instant, lifting him to his feet, tightening his fist for another punch.

"Don't hurt me!" the man cried, struggling in vain to break free. "Give me a chance, man. Give me a chance!"

"Did you give *him* a chance!" Peter screamed, his fury

boiling over. "The man you killed, did you give *him* a chance? *Did* you? *Answer* me!"

Peter pulled the man around, preparing to launch him across the building again when, for the first time, he caught a glimpse of the killer's face, illuminated by a police search-light.

Peter Parker recognized the man. There could no mistaking the platinum hair and beady eyes. This was the thief who had robbed the wrestling promoter earlier that evening. This was the man Peter had allowed to escape, when he could easily have stopped him. This was the same man who had just killed his beloved uncle Ben.

"No!" Peter cried, his chest tightening, his breathing strained. "No, not you! It can't be *you!*" He hurled the killer into a wall, where he slumped to the floor in a heap—right next to his fallen gun.

Peter buried his face in his hands as images flooded his mind—the red-faced promoter screaming that he had just been robbed; the platinum-haired thief racing toward the elevator clutching a bag full of money; the security guard calling out for Peter to stop the thief from getting away. And then the image of an angry, arrogant young man, too concerned with his own problems and a chance for petty revenge, standing by, allowing the thief to escape. One final image filled his head—the image of Uncle Ben's lifeless body sprawled on the street.

The killer scrambled to his feet, aiming his gun at Peter, who walked straight at him, seething with rage. The gunman pulled the trigger. A tinny click echoed in the huge, open building. The gun was empty.

Peter kept coming, chin down, fists clenched. The killer stumbled backward, still clutching the canvas bag. Then he tripped over an old piece of lumber and crashed through a low window.

Peter reached out to grab him, but was too late. The killer plunged to his death, crashing into a wooden dock fifty feet below. Loose bills from the open canvas bag fluttered to the ground all around him.

On the river, a police boat flashed its spotlight up to the window where Peter gazed down at the dead man's body.

"There's the other one!" an officer on the boat shouted to his partner, aiming his revolver at the illuminated figure in the window. "I told you there were two of them!"

The second officer raised his gun, but the figure in the window was gone.

On a stone gargoyle protruding from a nearby rooftop, Peter Parker sat, head in hands. The usual brash noise of New York City faded to near silence. The only sound in his head was that of his own low voice.

"Uncle Ben," he whispered, tears falling through his fingers onto his makeshift costume. "I'm so sorry. So very sorry."

After a long while, he stood and eased down the side of the building. Reaching the sidewalk, he headed for home, wondering how in the world he was going to break the news to Aunt May.

CHAPTER 12

T he testing grounds of Quest Aerospace stretched for miles in all directions, its perimeter defined by an end-less chain-link fence. In the center of this bleak, barren land-scape sat a concrete bunker half buried in the ground. On guard towers surrounding the bunker, armed security guards paced back and forth, scanning the horizon in all directions as high-powered searchlights lit up the night sky.

Inside the bunker a small group of military personnel, led by General Slocum, joined the coordinator of Quest's Project Badger, along with several other Quest employees.

"I think you're going to like this, General," the coordinator said, handing out binoculars to all present. "The Badger robot is the ultimate super-soldier. Take a look."

Peering through a long rectangular window, General Slocum and the others watched as a huge robot, standing over twelve feet tall, slowly approached an empty military truck. Raising its long metallic arms, the Badger fired rockets from the launchers built into each limb, blowing the truck into a million fiery pieces.

"I can see it's got firepower," the general said. "But what about its armor?"

"It exceeded all the stress tests we threw at it," the coordinator explained. "It can take a hit as well as dish out the punishment, General."

"I want to go over the budget figures," the general began. "But if it does what you say it can, I'll sign the contract to fund its production tomorrow."

The project coordinator pulled General Slocum aside. "What about your commitment to OsCorp?" he asked.

"Norman Osborn has done nothing but risk our time and money to satisfy his outrageous dreams," the general replied. "Nothing would please me more than to give his funding to you and put Osborn out of business."

A faint whine from outside the bunker grew louder. Rushing to the window, the group spotted something streaking across the night sky.

"What is that?" asked a Quest technician.

"I don't know," replied the coordinator. "But it's headed for the Badger."

The whine from outside reached an ear-shattering pitch. Then without warning, a rocket streaked from the sky, blowing the Badger to bits.

The security guards on the towers raised their weapons and unleashed a barrage of machine-gun fire, but they couldn't hit what they couldn't see, and the ghostly streak above them seemed to vanish, then reappear.

Additional rockets streaked from above, suddenly appearing just as they slammed into the towers, leveling them.

"What in blazes is going on?" General Slocum demanded, watching the massacre from inside the bunker.

His answer came in the form of screaming turbine engine and another high-pitched whine as a rocket headed right for the bunker.

"Oh, no," the general muttered, just as the bunker exploded in a brilliant ball of orange flames.

A green blur streaked over the smoking ruins of the bunker as a horrible cackle faded into the night.

The weeks following Uncle Ben's murder were the toughest of Peter Parker's life. He spent a lot of time at home, sticking close to Aunt May, trying to help her cope with the tragedy, while wrestling with his own guilt for having allowed it to happen.

On a bright June morning, the moment Peter Parker and his classmates had been waiting for finally arrived. Beaming students and proud parents filled an outdoor amphitheater for Midtown High School's graduation ceremonies. For Peter and his aunt it was a small break in the grief to celebrate a happy occasion, although Uncle Ben's absence lent a bittersweet flavor to the joyous proceedings.

Following the usual speeches and the handing out of diplomas, a time-honored tradition was carried out when hundreds of happy graduates flung their mortarboard hats high into the air. A great cheer exploded from the students. Then the crowd began to disperse as the happy graduates went off in search of their loved ones.

As he scanned the mob for Aunt May, Peter spotted Harry searching for his father.

"Hey, Harry!" Peter cried out joyfully. "We made it, buddy!"

"We sure did," Harry replied. "Thanks in no small part to you! So, I've got some good news. My father owns a building downtown with an empty loft. He said we could use it. Why not move in with me in the city?"

"I don't know," Peter said, shrugging. "I'm not sure I can afford the rent. I have to get a job first!"

"We'll work something out," Harry said, smiling.

A short distance away, May Parker and Norman Osborn waded through the sea of people, searching for their graduates. May recognized Norman.

"Mr. Osborn," she said, extending her right hand. "I'm May Parker, Peter's aunt."

"Aunt May," Norman said, grasping her hand warmly. "How do you do? I can't seem to find my boy."

"There's Harry," Aunt May said, pointing up and over the heads of the people standing next to her.

Harry broke through the crowd, clutching his diploma proudly. "Hey, Dad!" he cried, pausing before his father. He longed for a warm, parental embrace, but knew better than to expect one.

"You made it," Norman said, offering his hand. "It's not the first time I've been proven wrong. Congratulations."

"Thanks," Harry said, accepting his father's firm handshake.

"Congratulations, Harry," Aunt May added, hugging him tightly.

"Look who it is!" Norman cried, spotting Peter moving toward them. "The winner of the science award!"

Peter finally reached the others, stepping up to Aunt May, throwing his arms around her.

"Here's our graduate," she said, hugging Peter tightly, beaming with pride. "You two boys looked so handsome up there."

Norman put his hand on Peter's shoulder. "I know this has been a hard time for you," he said. "If you ever need anything . . ."

"Thanks, Mr. Osborn," Peter replied, nodding.

This was not the first time that Harry had gotten the feeling that his father liked Peter better than he liked him. Looking away from the touching scene, he spotted Mary Jane and Flash Thompson. They were arguing. M.J. shoved Flash away, then turned and pushed her way through the crowd. Harry glanced back at Peter and Norman, then ran toward M.J.

Later that afternoon, back at home, Peter headed up the stairs toward his room. Aunt May followed, worried that with the excitement of the day's festivities past, Peter's sadness would be greater than ever.

His door was ajar and she knocked gently, then stepped into his room, sitting next to him on the edge of his bed.

"I missed him a lot today," Peter said softly, staring down at the floor.

"I know," Aunt May replied, taking Peter's hand. "I miss him, too. But he was there. I could tell. He wouldn't have missed it."

Peter lifted his head and looked at the ceiling in exasperation. "I just wish I hadn't—"

"Peter, don't start that again," Aunt May cut him off.

"I can't stop thinking about the last thing I said to him," Peter went on, the torment showing in his voice.

"Stop torturing yourself," Aunt May said gently.

"He tried to tell me something important and I threw it back in his face," Peter said, his chin dropping to his chest once more.

"You loved him," Aunt May stated. "And he loved you. He never doubted the man you would grow into. He knew you were meant for great things. You won't disappoint him." Then squeezing his hand, she added, "Or me."

She got up quietly and left Peter to his own thoughts.

When he was alone, Peter slid open the bottom drawer of his dresser and pulled out the red-and-blue costume and mask that he had been working on for days. Black web lines ran throughout the red sections—chest, shoulders, gloves, boots, and mask—and a black spider sat in the center of the webbing on the chest. The mask had two white oval-shaped eye pieces, designed by Peter so that he could see out, but no one could see in.

Spreading the costume out on his bed, Peter heard Uncle Ben's voice fill his head.

"Remember," the warm, familiar voice said. "With great power comes great responsibility."

CHAPTER 13

Over the next few weeks, New York City was abuzz with reports of a strange blue-and-red-clad figure foiling criminals like a one-man wrecking crew. Unbelievable stories splashed across the front pages of the city's newspapers and flew from the lips of cabbies, construction workers, and the others who make up the varied fabric of the great tapestry that is New York.

A thief about to shoot a grocer had the gun plucked from his hand by a strand of sticky webbing streaking down from a shadowy figure.

Police arriving on the scene of a jewelry-store robbery found the three thieves neatly tied up in a sack made of webbing, dangling from nearby lamppost.

A woman whose purse was snatched saw the crook swept up into the sky in a blue-and-red blur, only to have her purse fall back into her hands with a note attached that read: *"COURTESY OF YOUR FRIENDLY NEIGHBORHOOD SPIDER-MAN"*

The police didn't know what to make of this masked, costumed crusader. Some thought him a hero, some an unwanted vigilante.

In the offices of New York's largest tabloid newspaper, the *Daily Bugle*, publisher J. Jonah Jameson knew exactly what to make of this so-called Spider-Man.

"He's a criminal!" Jameson shouted to Robbie Robertson, his longtime editor-in-chief. "A public menace! What's he doing on my front page?"

Jameson tossed the day's edition of the *Bugle* down on his desk, revealing its headline: WHO IS SPIDER-MAN? COSTUMED FIGURE SAVES FIRE VICTIMS. Beside the headline sat a photograph of a burning building, with a blurry figure crawling up its side.

"He's news, boss," Robertson explained. "He saved six people from burning to death."

"He probably started the fire!" Jameson shot back. "Something goes wrong and this creepy crawler's right there? What's that tell you, huh?"

"That he's a hero," Robertson replied.

"Then why does he wear a mask?" Jameson shouted. "What's he got to hide?"

A broad smile spread across Robertson's face. After all these years he could read his boss like a book. He saved his best shot for last. "We sold out all four printings of today's paper, Jonah," he said.

"Sold out?" Jameson asked.

"Every copy," Robertson replied, savoring the moment.

"I want Spider-Man on page one tomorrow!" Jameson shouted. "With a decent picture this time!"

"That's the real problem," Robertson explained. "We can't get a good picture. I've had Eddie Brock out trying to get a shot of this guy for weeks, but nobody ever catches more than a glimpse of him."

"What is he, shy?" Jameson yelled, pounding his fist on the desk. "He doesn't want to be famous? Put an ad on the front page. 'Cash paid for a picture of Spider-Man!' Someone will get a shot of him, I guarantee it."

"Maybe he doesn't want to be famous, boss," Robertson suggested.

"Fine!" Jameson railed. "Then I'll make him infamous!"

Peter Parker raced across the campus of Empire State University in Manhattan. Since he had started college, it felt as if he was always late for something—classes, appointments, dinner. Trying to juggle his life as a student and a superhero, not to mention trying to earn a few bucks, left him wishing for more hours in the day.

As he dashed into the university's science building, his fingers swiftly buttoned his shirt, hiding the red-and-blue costume beneath.

"Dr. Connors!" Peter shouted, spotting the one-armed professor walking down the hall.

"You're an hour late, Parker," Dr. Curt Connors said, sighing and shaking his head. "Class is over. You missed another session."

"I'm sorry," Peter blurted out. "It won't—"

"Look, Peter," Dr. Connors continued. "You have a great scientific mind, but you can't seem to get your priorities straight. You've been late six times this semester."

"Professor, please let me explain," Peter begged.

"This is a paid internship," Dr. Connors went on, ignoring Peter's plea. "Do you know how many freshmen applied for it? Do you know how many would even do it for free!"

"Dr. Connors," Peter tried one last time. "I need this job!"

The professor placed his hand on Peter's shoulder. "I like you, Peter," he said with genuine warmth. "Come see me when you grow up a little."

Peter walked slowly from the science building and wandered off the campus out onto the streets of Manhattan. He had been counting on this internship. Now he would have to find another way to make money, another way to pay Harry his share of the rent.

Strolling past a grungy-looking diner, Peter noticed a woman storm out its front door, the sound of shouting trailing behind her. It was Mary Jane.

"Hey!" he called, running up behind her.

"Buzz off!" M.J. shouted, not bothering to turn around.

"M.J., it's me, Peter," he called.

Mary Jane stopped and turned. "What are you up to?" she asked.

"I just lost my job," Peter admitted. "I've got to find another one. What about you?"

"I, um," M.J. stammered. "I'm headed for an audition."

"So, you're acting, now," Peter said enthusiastically. "That's great!"

"Yeah," M.J. replied flatly, her head down. "It's a dream come true."

The door to the diner burst open and a large man came racing up behind them. He was wearing an apron, and he clutched a stack of restaurant checks in his beefy fist.

"Hey, miss actress," he shouted at M.J. "You're off by six bucks. Next time I take it out of your check, miss waitress!" Then he turned and stormed back into the diner.

"It's just temporary," M.J. explained, unable to hide her embarrassment. "A few extra dollars."

"It's nothing to be embarrassed about," Peter replied quickly. "I've been fired from worse jobs than that!"

"Please don't tell Harry," M.J. blurted out.

"Harry?" Peter asked, baffled at the mention of his roommate's name.

"We've been going out," M.J. said, puzzled. "Didn't he tell you? Aren't you guys living in the same apartment?"

"Oh, yeah, right," Peter said, trying to cover his surprise.

"I think he'd hate the idea of me waiting on tables," M.J. explained. "He'd think it was beneath me."

"Well, Harry has never really lived on a little place I like to call planet Earth," Peter joked.

Mary Jane laughed. "How come you always know how to make me feel better?" she asked, squeezing Peter's hand. "So long, Pete."

"See ya," Peter said. "And don't worry. I won't tell Harry."

"Thanks," she replied, then she turned the corner and disappeared down the block.

Peter stopped and looked to the sky, shaking his head. "Harry and Mary Jane, wow!" he muttered. He dropped his head and walked toward home.

Stepping into the spacious loft he shared with Harry Osborn, Peter noticed his roommate sitting at a desk, studying. Norman Osborn paced the length of the loft, speaking into a cellular phone. He nodded at Peter, who returned the gesture.

"Typical," Harry said as Peter slumped down on the couch. "Dad comes to visit and spends all his time on the phone."

Then he noticed Peter's expression. "What's wrong with you?"

"I was late and Dr. Connors fired me," Peter explained.

"Late again?" Harry asked. "Where do you go all the time?"

Peter shrugged. "Around," he mumbled. Keeping his life as Spider-Man a secret from those he cared about was a major concern these days.

Norman Osborn finished his phone call and turned to Peter. "Hello, Peter," he said. "Maybe *you* can tell me who this mystery girl is, the one Harry's been dating. He wants me to meet this one. That's a first."

"Dad!" Harry whined.

"Sorry, Mr. Osborn," Peter said, looking straight at Harry. "Harry hasn't mentioned her."

"Hey, Dad, Pete's looking for work," Harry blurted out, happy to change the subject. "Why don't you give him a job?"

"No, that's not necessary, sir," Peter said quickly. "I appreciate it, but I'll be fine. I'll find something."

"What kind of work are you looking for, Peter?" Norman asked.

"I'm thinking of something in photography, actually," Peter replied, picking up the *Daily Bugle*, which had been folded on the coffee table. Peter intended to flip to the classified ads to begin his job search, but the image on the *Bugle*'s front page stopped him cold.

A crude sketch of Spider-Man's masked face stared out at him from page one. Above it the headline read: WANTED: PHOTOGRAPHIC PROOF! DOES SPIDER-MAN REALLY EXIST? PROVE IT TO US. REWARD OFFERED! WILL PAY CASH!

CHAPTER 14

That night, Spider-Man clung to the third-floor window ledge of a bank downtown. Hiding in the darkness above the streetlights, he worked quickly. He knew that a robbery was in progress in the bank below. He also knew that he had only one chance to get this right.

Lining his lens up so its focus was on the bank's entrance below, he attached the camera to the bottom of the window ledge using a glob of sticky webbing. Listening carefully, Spider-Man waited for the robbers to make their exit.

A commotion broke out at the door. As three bank robbers emerged, Spider-Man hit the automatic shutter release button on his camera, then leaped into action.

Swinging down on a web line, he slammed into the robbers, just as the flash on his camera started to go off. During the short struggle that followed, the camera shot a series of pictures of Spider-Man in action.

Finally bundling the burglars in a web sack—complete with a note for the police—Spider-Man scrambled up the front of the building, retrieved his camera, then slipped away into the night.

Peter Parker takes pictures for the school newspaper.

The students learn about mutant spiders.

Peter discovers his newfound powers.

Peter is faster and stronger than ever!

The amazing Spider-Man leaps straight up to avoid Bone Saw's crushing fists.

Spider-Man is the winner!

Peter moves to the city with his friend Harry.

The Green Goblin makes his first appearance at the World Unity Day festival.

WHAM! Spider-Man unleashes a powerful punch.

Rising from the smoke, the Green Goblin soars on his glider after Spider-Man.

M.J. clings tightly to Spider-Man as he lowers her to safety.

The Green Goblin reveals his true self to Spider-Man—Norman Osborne!

Spider-Man lives by Uncle Ben's advice: With great power comes great responsibility.

The next morning at the offices of the *Daily Bugle*, Peter Parker handed a stack of photos to Robbie Robertson.

Flipping through the shots of Spider-Man web-swinging and battling the burglars, Robbie nodded his head and smiled. "They're good," he said to Peter. "They're very good. How'd you get them?"

"If I tell you, you'll send your own photographer," Peter said, smiling right back at Robbie. "Am I hired?"

"It's not up to me," Robbie explained, shrugging. "Mr. Jameson hires all staff personally."

At that moment a young man with a camera around his neck burst out of Jameson's office. His clothes were disheveled, his hair uncombed, and his face spoke of unimaginable terrors in the office beyond.

Jameson's voice came booming from the open doorway. "I said get me a picture, Eddie!" he screamed. "Not an inkblot! Why can't anyone get me a decent picture of that costumed freak? Now get out of here, Eddie!"

Robbie looked at Peter as Eddie shuffled toward the exit. "Mr. Jameson fires all staff personally, as well," he said, raising his eyebrows.

Jameson stormed out of his office, still yelling. "And Eddie," he blustered. "Would it kill you to get a decent suit!"

Eddie ran from the room, leaving Jameson to turn his attention to Peter. "What!" he shouted at the hopeful young man before him.

"This guy's got some shots of Spider-Man, boss," Robbie explained.

"Well, don't just stand there," Jameson yelled. "Bring them in."

Peter and Robbie followed Jameson into his office. The publisher grabbed the pictures from Robbie's hand and flipped through them, slamming each one down onto his desk, after viewing it.

"Crap!" he muttered, after looking at the first picture.

"Crap! Crap! Crap!" he repeated after the second, third, and fourth.

Peter looked at Robbie, who winked at him conspiratorially.

"They're all crap," Jameson said when he had finished looking. The last thing he wanted to do was encourage a rookie photographer by offering him top dollar. Especially one who brought him terrific shots like these. "I'll give you three hundred for all of them."

Peter, emboldened by Robbie's gesture and the knowledge that nobody else could possibly get these shots, spoke softly but firmly. "That seems a little low," he said.

"Fine," snapped Jameson. "Then take them somewhere else."

Peter gathered up the photos and turned to leave.

"Wait," Jameson ordered, hating the fact that this novice had called his bluff. "All right, I'll give you five hundred. That's the standard freelance fee."

Peter agreed, handing the shots back to Jameson, who passed them on to Robbie.

"Tear up page one," Jameson whispered, pointing to a photo of Spider-Man battling the burglars. "Run that shot instead."

Wow! Peter thought. *Page one! I should have held out for more money!*

"Headline?" Robbie asked his boss.

"Spider-Man: Hero or Menace? Exclusive *Daily Bugle* Photos!" Jameson blurted out without a moment's hesitation.

"Menace?" Peter asked, shaking his head. "Sir, he was stopping that robbery and capturing those—"

"What are you, his lawyer?" Jameson barked back. "You take the pictures, I write the headlines. Is that all right with you?"

"Yes, sir," Peter replied, realizing his argument would get him nowhere. Then he quickly added, "I would like a staff job, sir."

"No jobs!" Jameson shouted back. "Freelance is the best thing for a kid your age. Bring me some more shots of that newspaper-selling clown and I just might take them off your hands."

Peter nodded at Jameson, winked at Robbie in a gesture of thanks, then turned and strode quickly from the office.

Over the next few weeks, using his webbed-up camera with its automatic shutter, Peter got one great shot after another of Spider-Man in action. Each time, Jameson gladly bought the photos and ran them on the *Bugle*'s front page.

But despite the images of Spider-Man foiling robberies, rescuing people from burning buildings, and stopping muggers from preying on innocent victims, Jameson continued his campaign of attacking Spider-Man. Headlines like: NY FEARS COSTUMED COWARD!, SPIDER-MAN: SUPER-HERO OR SUPER-ZERO?, and BIG APPLE FEARS SPIDER BITE! screamed out from the newspaper's front page, day after day, accompanied by Peter's photos.

The constant barrage of negative press bothered Peter a

great deal. It grew tougher and tougher to spend his nights fighting crime as Spider-Man, only to see his actions turned around and misinterpreted the next day in the *Bugle*.

"Why are you so hard on him?" Peter asked Jameson one morning while dropping off his latest batch of Spidey shots.

"He thinks he's the law," Jameson replied. "There's no place in this society for vigilante justice. Once one person takes the law into his own hands, pretty soon you've got anarchy."

Not satisfied with Jameson's response, Peter spoke up. "Mr. Jameson," he began cautiously. "I'd like an assignment shooting something other than Spider-Man."

"No," barked Jameson. "Just keep doing what you're doing."

"Jonah," Robbie said, stepping in. "Let's send Peter to cover the OsCorp World Unity Festival. We've got to send someone."

"World Unity Festival," Jameson grumbled. "What a joke. Another display of Norman Osborn's giant ego. Fine. Send Peter. Now go get me some pictures!"

"Yes, sir," Peter replied, smiling at Robbie, who had once again stood up for him against his blustery boss.

The Manhattan headquarters of OsCorp Industries rose like a giant medieval tower in the jagged New York skyline. In the board room, high above the city streets, Norman Osborn addressed the board of directors.

"I am pleased to announce," he began in his usual smug, self-righteous tone, "that as of today, OsCorp Industries has passed Quest Aerospace as the leading supplier to the

United States military. Since the tragic attack at Quest, our costs have gone down, our revenue has gone up, and our stock has never been higher."

Mr. Balkan looked around at his fellow board members. Clearing his throat, he turned to Norman. "That's wonderful news," he announced. "In fact, it's the reason we're selling the company."

The blood drained from Osborn's face, turning his skin pale. His eyes narrowed and he swallowed hard. "What?" he cried out. "I don't understand."

"Quest Aerospace has obtained new financing in the wake of the attack," Balkan explained calmly. "They are buying OsCorp."

"You can't do this," Norman stammered. "I built this company!"

Mr. Fargas spoke next, turning his wheelchair to face Osborn. "In fact, Norman," he began. "They want you out. This board expects your resignation within thirty days."

"Fargas, please," Norman pleaded. "Don't do this."

"I'm sorry, Norman," Fargas replied. "The board is unanimous on this. We're announcing the sale right after the World Unity Festival. You're out."

"Am I?" Norman replied, a menacing tone creeping into his voice. "We'll just see about that!"

CHAPTER 15

A huge crowd gathered in Times Square, surrounded by brightly colored flags and banners announcing the World Unity Festival. A large globe hung overhead, a symbol of the gathering organized by OsCorp. The official theme of the day was worldwide healing and a coming together of all people.

Giant balloons floated over the crowd. The thousands who had come out on this beautiful morning enjoyed music, jugglers, and clowns, along with cotton candy and other sweet goodies.

Five stories above the crowd, the balcony of an old building had been converted into a reviewing stand, a special private place for dignitaries and those with the right connections to sit and view the day's proceedings.

Among the many V.I.P.s and invited guests on the reviewing stand were the nine men and women of the OsCorp Industries board of directors. Nearby, Harry Osborn sat with his date, Mary Jane Watson. Harry was hoping to finally introduce M.J. to his father, but so far there was no sign of

Norman Osborn, the man who had come up with the idea for Unity Day in the first place.

Down on the street, Peter Parker made his way through the throng of people, shooting pictures of the crowd, the balloons, the banners, anything he spotted that captured the joyous, celebratory atmosphere of the event.

Peering through his lens, Peter's view swung past the reviewing stand, just as Harry tried to kiss M.J. She turned away to avoid the attempt. Peter's mind filled with hope. Maybe Harry and M.J. weren't as serious as he had thought.

At that moment Harry glanced in his direction, and the two friends realized that they were staring at each other. Peter felt embarrassed, as did Harry. Then, instantly, something blotted all other thoughts and feelings from Peter's mind.

His spider sense went off like crazy. The overwhelming sensation that something terrible was about to happen crowded out everything else. Lowering his camera, Peter scanned the area, but saw nothing out of the ordinary among the happy congregation of people.

Up on the reviewing stand, Harry approached Mr. Fargas and Mr. Balkan. "Have either of you seen my father?" Harry asked the two board members.

Balkan and Fargas exchanged uncomfortable glances. "I'm not sure he'll be joining us," Fargas replied, rolling his wheelchair away from Harry.

Fargas stopped suddenly and looked up, searching the sky for the source of a high-pitched whine coming from overhead. "What is that?" Fargas cried, spotting a blur tearing across the sky.

Peter gazed up and saw a green streak moving quickly, darting in and out of the clouds.

On the reviewing stand, Mr. Balkan raised his binoculars. "Must be a new gimmick for this year's festival," he said, looking through the lenses. "As if this thing doesn't cost us enough money already." Spotting a figure riding atop a familiar shape, Balkan cried, "What is going on! Is that our Flying Wing? The one that was stolen from the lab?"

The figure, clad all in green, swooped back around in an arc, then paused, hovering above the reviewing stand. Balkan and Fargas looked at each other, concern showing on their faces. Not only was this green character riding their experimental flying wing, but he was also wearing the special electronic suit OsCorp had developed to control the one-person glider.

The strange-looking figure wore a grotesque green mask that hid his face completely. The mask twisted into a hideous, demonic grin, giving the impression of a monstrous Halloween goblin.

This Green Goblin, as the press came to call him in the days that followed, pulled a small, round, pumpkin-shaped object from his belt. The crowd cheered enthusiastically at this new, if slightly bizarre, addition to the festivities.

The Green Goblin moved his arm slightly and the glider responded instantly, sending him flying in a tight circle right in front of the reviewing stand.

Shrieks of laughter turned to cries of terror as the Goblin tossed the strange pumpkin-shaped object onto the reviewing stand.

Foooomm!

The pumpkin bomb detonated, blowing away half the stand. Large chunks of wood and concrete rained down onto the street, scattering the startled crowd and sending the performers racing for cover. Panic spread as people quickly realized that the Green Goblin was by no means part of the show.

The remaining piece of the reviewing stand lurched downward, sending dignitaries toppling to the ground, five stories below. Mary Jane fell forward, landing near the edge of the stand, while Harry toppled backward, several feet away from her.

Down on the street, Peter pushed his way through the crowd, desperately trying to reach a nearby alley.

With a sickening crunch, the reviewing stand pulled farther away from the building to which it had been anchored, dropping several feet. Mary Jane tumbled closer to the end of the balcony, her head dangling over the edge. Staring down at the mayhem below, she saw the crowd frantically scrambling for safety.

With a simple move of his right wrist, the Green Goblin accelerated into the sky, cackling with delight. He circled the screaming crowd, pleased with the effect his handiwork was having.

Sweeping past the reviewing stand again, the Green Goblin tossed another pumpkin bomb, which landed at the feet of the OsCorp board of directors.

Foooomm!

The second pumpkin bomb detonated, instantly vaporizing

the nine men and women who had just put Norman Osborn out of a job. The unsteady balcony shook and crumbled even more.

The Green Goblin dropped his left shoulder slightly and the glider's nose dipped down, sending the turbo-charged flying wing zooming below the reviewing stand.

On the crumbling balcony, Harry crawled toward Mary Jane, who clutched the edge of the sloping stand to keep from falling off. Just before he reached her, Harry watched in horror as the Green Goblin rose slowly, hovering in midair, unleashing a blood-curdling cackle as he reached for M.J.'s arm.

A red-and-blue figure swung down from above, feet first, slamming into the Goblin, knocking him from his glider. "I don't know who you are, mister," Spider-Man quipped as he landed on the side of a building. "But this town is big enough for only one costumed weirdo. And that guy is me!"

"It's Spider-Man!" came cries from the crowd below. "He just whacked that green creep."

"Yeah!" shouted another spectator. "Spider-Man! I saw his picture in the paper."

Spider-Man looked around, assessing the situation. He spotted Mary Jane on the edge of the reviewing stand, only inches from plunging to her doom. He was about to swing over and scoop her off the teetering platform when screams from the street caught his attention.

The Green Goblin crashed into a large tent, breaking his fall. Pressing a button on the wrist of his electronic suit, he signaled the glider, which came soaring down toward him. Before it reached the Green Goblin, however, the speeding glider slammed into the giant World Unity Festival globe, knocking it from its support perch.

The massive sphere rolled down the middle of the street, crushing everything in its path. Completely out of control and totally unstoppable, the globe headed straight for a six-year-old boy, who stood frozen with fear, clutching a wand of cotton candy.

Firing a web at a nearby billboard, Spider-Man swung down in a tight arc, scooping the child into his arms and rising up out of danger just as the globe barrelled by, demolishing a line of parking meters.

"One special-delivery package for you, ma'am," Spider-Man said, depositing the boy safely at his mother's side. Looking back, he saw five police officers, guns drawn, surrounding the Green Goblin, who had untangled himself from the collapsed tent.

"Don't shoot! I surrender!" the Green Goblin cried, raising his hands into the air. "It's not my fault. Media violence made me do it!" Then he charged into the group of cops, who tackled the Green Goblin and wrestled him to the ground.

Spider-Man glanced back up at Mary Jane and was about to leap up and get her off the balcony when he heard screams coming from the startled officers. He watched as, with an astounding burst of strength, the Goblin tossed the officers off as if they were rag dolls. M.J. would literally have to hang in there for a little while longer.

Leaping high in the air, somersaulting over the crowd, Spider-Man landed in front of the Green Goblin.

"How dare you interfere with me!" the Goblin snarled at his costumed adversary. "What do you want?"

"World peace," Spider-Man shot back. "But I'll settle for your chin."

Wham!

Spider-Man unleashed a powerful punch right to the Green Goblin's chin, sending him flying into a nearby building. Leaping to the Green Goblin's side, the web swinger threw another punch. This time, a green gloved hand seized Spider-Man's fist, stopping its forward motion.

"See what I did there?" the Goblin cackled, letting loose a punch of his own.

Spider-Man tumbled through the air, knocking over an ice-cream vendor's cart and crashing into a lamppost.

The Green Goblin pressed a small button on his wrist, and once again his glider streaked toward him. Leaping on, he soared into the air as Spider-Man jumped to his feet.

The Green Goblin banked sharply to the left, then turned back toward Spider-Man, who spotted two small machine guns descending from the glider's bottom. The machine guns fired, raking the ground near Spidey, who leaped onto a nearby balloon as the Green Goblin disappeared into the clouds.

Hanging on only by a handful of remaining rivets, the reviewing stand creaked loudly, inching closer to the ground. The sound caught Spider-Man's attention as he balanced on top of the giant balloon. There were five more balloons between him and the crumbling balcony. In a red-and-blue blur, Spider-Man bounced from balloon to balloon.

He leaped for the balcony, but the Green Goblin appeared from nowhere, grabbing Spider-Man around the waist and slamming him into a wall above the wrecked platform.

Spider-Man tumbled onto the stand, landing near Mary Jane, as debris rained down all around them. A chunk of wood struck Harry on the head, knocking him unconscious.

Spider-Man stepped toward M.J. just as the Green Goblin rose on his glider and hovered above the reviewing stand. A laser weapon sprung from the glider's side, aimed right at Spider-Man.

With lightning speed, Spider-Man shot a glob of sticky webbing at the Green Goblin. It splattered across his face, blocking his vision.

"No!" screamed the Green Goblin, firing his laser. The searing beam missed its target, slamming into the wall behind Spider-Man. Using his incredible strength, Spider-Man punched a hole in the bottom of the Green Goblin's glider. Reaching in, he tore out a fistful of wiring.

Smoking and sputtering, the glider zoomed away, with the Green Goblin desperately trying to pull the webbing from his eyes.

Spider-Man breathed a sigh of relief. At that moment, what was left of the reviewing stand split in two, tossing Mary Jane over the edge.

Harry's eyes popped open. He was up on the piece of the reviewing stand that remained attached to the building. He watched in stunned amazement as Spider-Man dove after M.J., launching himself into a headfirst free-fall, trailing a web strand behind him. Catching up with her just inches above the pavement, Spider-Man caught M.J. by the waist as his web line pulled taut, stopping their fall.

Swinging away just as the empty piece of balcony crashed to the street, Spider-Man and Mary Jane rose high above the scene of destruction. Smoothly web-swinging among the skyscrapers and realizing that they were finally out of danger, Spider-Man looked at M.J.

"You all right?" he asked as he fired another web strand.

"Who are you?" Mary Jane asked, still in shock from her narrow escape. This airborne journey among the city's tallest buildings felt like a strange dream.

"You know who I am," Spider-Man replied, gently landing on the rooftop garden of Rockefeller Center, then removing his arm from M.J.'s waist.

"I do?" she answered, still baffled by the whole experience.

Spider-Man stepped to the edge of the roof. "Sure," he said, firing a web strand. "I'm your friendly neighborhood Spider-Man!" Then he leaped from the roof, swinging off into the concrete canyons of midtown Manhattan.

CHAPTER 16

That evening in their apartment, Peter casually drank a glass of milk as Harry frantically called Mary Jane, leaving message after message, hoping she was all right. Harry had regained consciousness in time to watch, along with the stunned crowd, as the strange man in red and blue swooped in and saved M.J.

But Harry read the *Daily Bugle* like most New Yorkers, and he now wondered if this Spider-Man guy was really on the side of good, or just some maniac in a costume—a maniac that had swung off with his girlfriend!

"I hope M.J. calls soon," Harry said, pacing the living room floor. "I'm really worried."

"She will," Peter replied calmly, drinking down a big gulp of milk.

"How do you know?" Harry asked.

"Just a feeling I have," Peter said. "How's your head?"

"They patched it up," Harry explained. "It's nothing. Why aren't you worried about M.J.?"

The phone rang and Harry grabbed it.

"Hiya," M.J. said in a light, distracted voice.

"Are you all right?" Harry shouted into the phone. "Did he hurt you?"

"Of course not," Mary Jane replied, laughing softly. "He was wonderful, incredible!"

"What do you mean, he was incredible?" Harry shot back. "Where did he take you?"

"To the Rockefeller Center roof garden," Mary Jane said dreamily. "Have you ever been there? It's so romantic!"

"No, I haven't been there," Harry said sharply. "Look, I'm coming over."

"No," M.J. replied quickly. "I'm exhausted. I'm going to sleep."

"Well, call me when you wake up," Harry said. "We'll go have breakfast or something. Okay? Bye."

Harry hung up the phone. Peter had only heard Harry's half of the conversation, but it was enough make him smile broadly.

"Look, Peter," Harry began uncomfortably. "About that picture you took with M.J. and me."

"It's okay," Peter replied. "I didn't take it."

"I know I should have told you about us," Harry began. "I'm crazy about her."

"I'm your friend," Peter replied. "You didn't have to lie."

"I always knew you wanted to go out with her," Harry went on. "But you never made a move, never said anything to her."

"I guess I didn't," Peter said, thinking of all the chances he'd passed up.

"Well, I'm still shaking from today," Harry said, heading to his bedroom. "What was that thing that attacked us?"

"I don't know," Peter said grimly. "But somebody has to stop it!"

Norman Osborn stood in the open doorway of his apartment, clutching a copy of the *Daily Bugle* in his hands. It was the morning after the attack on the World Unity Festival, and Osborn had been wandering the streets all night. His clothes were a mess and dark bags rimmed the bottoms of his sleepless eyes.

Glancing down at the *Bugle*'s front page, Osborn read the headline that ran above a photo of Spider-Man battling the Green Goblin: SPIDER-MAN, GREEN GOBLIN TERRORIZE CITY!

Osborn shook his head, trying to make sense of the words, images of the terror at the festival flashing through his mind. Looking down the page another headline caught his attention: OSCORP BOARD MEMBERS KILLED!

Osborn stumbled into his apartment and up the stairs toward his study. From somewhere in the apartment a low, menacing, cackling sounded.

"Is somebody there?" Osborn called out. He was met with silence. "No, of course not."

Stepping into his study, Osborn tossed the newspaper onto his desk, then slipped off his suit jacket. He slumped into his desk chair.

The bizarre, otherworldly laughter came again, growing louder, and finally speaking. "Stop pretending, Norman," said the eerie yet somehow familiar voice.

"Who is that?" Osborn cried, looking around, but seeing no one. "Where are you?"

97

"Just follow the cold shiver running down your spine," replied the ghostly voice. "Look, I'm right here."

Still, Osborn saw no one. Where could that voice be coming from? He moaned, grasping his head with his hands. It felt as if the voice was coming from all around him, or maybe from inside his own head.

"Did you think it was coincidence that so many good things have all happened just for you, Norman?" the shrill voice asked from everywhere and nowhere at the same time.

"What do you want?" Osborn shouted, throwing his head back, raging at this unseen intruder.

"To say what you won't," the voice responded. "To do what you can't. To remove those in your way."

Osborn snapped his head forward, his mind focusing more sharply now. "You killed the board members?" Osborn asked, no longer concerned about where the intruder was located.

"*We* killed them, Norman," the voice responded, sounding closer than ever.

"No!" Osborn raged. "I would never do that!"

"You sicken me with your weakness," the voice cackled.

"I'm not a murderer!" Norman yelled, leaping to his feet. "I'm a scientist, a respectable businessman!"

"Shut up and listen to the beauty of this, Norman," the voice boomed with a deafening shriek. "You are now in full control of OsCorp Industries. Your greatest wish, granted by me. Say 'Thank you.'"

A strange calm came over Norman. His mind moved swiftly, pieces falling into place. "What's next?" he asked.

"We'll eliminate your rivals," the voice began in a tone of

self-satisfaction. "OsCorp will become the most powerful military supplier in history. You can take what you've always wanted, Norman. Power!"

Osborn slipped his jacket back on and moved to a mirror. Straightening his hair and buttoning his shirt, he began to compose himself, once more just a businessman preparing for another meeting. "We can't do it alone," he stated calmly, at last accepting the ghostly voice as a partner, and maybe something more.

"There is only one who could stop us," the eerie voice said.

"Or he could be our greatest ally," Osborn replied, completely at peace with the voice that was now clearly coming from inside his head.

"Exactly!" cried the voice—the voice of the Green Goblin. "We need to have a little chat with Spider-Man."

Osborn snatched the *Daily Bugle* from his desk and looked again at the photo on the front page. "And I know exactly how we'll find him!"

CHAPTER 17

"**T**he Green Goblin!" J. Jonah Jameson announced proudly, holding the *Bugle*'s front page at arm's length. Jameson sat at his desk chomping on a cigar, glancing over the top of the paper at Peter Parker, who paced back and forth across the office. "You like the name? I made it up myself. Ever since Spider-Man, they all have to have a fancy name."

Peter read the headline teaming Spider-Man with the Green Goblin and shook his head. "Spider-Man wasn't terrorizing the city," he said. "He was trying to save it! That's slander!"

"Slander is spoken," Jameson corrected Peter. "In print, it's called libel. So let him sue me like a normal person!"

Peter realized that continuing the argument would be useless. He turned and walked from the office. As he left, he heard a vaguely familiar high-pitched whine, muffled by the glass of the sealed office window.

Ka-rash!

The Green Goblin exploded through the window behind

Jameson, shards of glass scattering everywhere. His glider paused above Jameson's desk. The Green Goblin grabbed the *Bugle*'s publisher by the throat with one hand, lifting him out of his chair. Jameson dangled helplessly above the floor, gasping for breath.

"Where is the photographer who takes the pictures of Spider-Man?" the Green Goblin asked in his thin, ghostly voice. "I need to talk to him about his favorite subject."

Peter had already disappeared down the hallway as the *Bugle*'s employees scrambled to safety.

"He's a freelancer!" Jameson replied, his voice choked and strained from the green-gloved hand that closed around his windpipe. "I don't know who he is. His stuff comes in the mail."

"You're lying!" the Green Goblin screeched. "Now I'll give you one last chance to tell me."

"Please," Jameson gasped. "Air. Can't breathe."

"Hey!" shouted a voice from behind the Green Goblin.

The Green Goblin spun around and saw Spider-Man hanging upside-down in the shattered window.

"I wear the tights in this town, bud," Spider-Man quipped.

"Speak of the devil!" the Green Goblin exclaimed, an evil grin spreading across his hideous green face. He released Jameson, who collapsed to the floor, gasping for air.

"I knew it!" Jameson exclaimed, wheezing and coughing. "You two are in this together! I knew that creep was—"

Thwip! Splat!

Spider-Man fired a small glob of webbing that landed on Jameson's mouth, sealing it shut. "Hey, kiddo, let Mom and

Dad here talk for a minute, will you?" Spider-Man said. For Peter Parker behind the mask, this was a moment of great satisfaction.

The Green Goblin reached his arm out toward Spider-Man and sprayed a stream of green gas from his glove.

Spider-Man grew dizzy, then blacked out completely, tumbling from the high window ledge, plunging toward the sidewalk below.

"Hate to beat and run, but I gotta go!" said the Green Goblin, firing up the turbo jets on his glider and zooming out the window.

Down he swooped, trailing flames and smoke behind him. Seconds before Spider-Man hit the ground, the Green Goblin caught him, then flew off into the darkness.

Consciousness returned slowly to Spider-Man. When he finally opened his eyes, the Green Goblin was staring down at him, smiling. Spider-Man pulled himself up into a sitting position, his body weak and heavy, every movement a struggle. Looking around, he saw that they were on a deserted rooftop, high above the city.

"Relax," the Green Goblin said. "My hallucinogenic gas slowed your central nervous system, but just for a few minutes. Long enough for us to have a talk."

"Who are you?" Spider-Man moaned, shifting his weight, trying to get comfortable and shake off the grogginess.

"A kindred spirit," the Green Goblin replied. "You've changed from what you once were, and now nobody could possibly understand what you're going through. Nobody, that is, except me. They call us freaks. But in truth, we are more than human, not less."

"I'm not like you," Spider-Man said. "You're a murderer."

"Well, to each his own," the Green Goblin replied. "You have chosen the path of the hero. But how long before the people of this city begin to hate you? Read the headlines. The day will come when you ask yourself why you risk your life for a bunch of ungrateful fools."

"Because it's the right thing to do," Spider-Man said, his head clearing slightly. He was still too weak to risk a battle with this powerful adversary. "It's the only thing to do."

"You and I, we are exceptional," the Green Goblin went on. "I had problems, but I used my extraordinary powers and quickly those problems vanished."

Spider-Man stared in silence. The Green Goblin continued.

"Imagine what we could accomplish working together. Think of what we could create. On the other hand, if we continue this senseless, selfish battle, countless innocents will die. And eventually, so will we."

The Green Goblin leaped onto his waiting glider. "Think about it, hero," he said. Then, with a tiny shrug of his shoulder, he streaked off into the darkness, his unearthly cackle fading into the night.

The following evening, fully recovered from the Green Goblin's gas attack, Peter Parker leaned against a brick wall outside the back of a downtown theater. Nearby, a door labeled ARTISTS ONLY opened quickly and out stepped Mary Jane, slamming the door hard behind her.

"Hey, how was the audition?" Peter asked, falling into stride next to her.

"How did you know?" M.J. asked, glad for his company.

"The official hotline," Peter replied. "Your mom told my aunt."

"So you just came by?" M.J. asked, flattered by the attention.

"I was in the neighborhood," Peter said. "I needed to see a friendly face. I took two buses to *get* to the neighborhood, but—"

"They told me I needed acting lessons," M.J. blurted out. "Can you believe that? A *soap opera* told me I needed acting lessons."

"Come on, I'll buy you a burger," Peter said hopefully.

Mary Jane smiled and took his hand. "I'd like that, but I can't," she said. "I'm having dinner with Harry. Why don't you join us?"

"No, thanks," Peter replied, shrugging his shoulders. "So, how's it going with you two?"

"Why so interested?" M.J. asked.

"I'm not interested," Peter replied, regretting the words as soon he said them.

"You're not?" M.J. asked, slightly confused.

"Well, why would I be?" Peter replied, digging himself a deeper hole.

"I don't know," she said. "Why would you be?"

Peter was growing more uncomfortable by the second.

"Sorry you won't come with us," Mary Jane said, breaking the silence. "I gotta run."

As M.J. disappeared down the street, Peter stared after her, kicking himself. Did he blow it again? Did she want him to confess his love for her, right there, right then?

His thoughts were interrupted by four young toughs who walked past him from behind, bumping him intentionally.

"Excuse *me*," Peter said sarcastically, shaken from his thoughts. The punks ignored him. Peter started off in the opposite direction, then glanced back over his shoulder at the four retreating tough guys. Something told him to follow them.

As Mary Jane turned a corner up ahead, the four punks caught up with her.

"Hey, pretty lady," one said, as the four surrounded her. "What's in your purse?"

A second punk grabbed for her bag.

"Beat it, sleazeballs!" she shouted, kicking one punk in the shins, elbowing another in the face, while spraying the remaining two with a canister of Mace which hung on her key chain. "What are you guys, from out of town or something?"

Recovering from M.J.'s surprising acts of self-defense, the four punks, furious now, gathered themselves and moved toward her menacingly. The mugger who had spoken reached into his pocket and pulled out a knife, snapping it open with an ominous *Snick!*

"That's it, pretty lady," he grumbled, raising the sharp blade toward M.J.'s face. "Playtime is over!"

"Actually," said a voice from the darkness above. "It's just begun!"

Thwip! Swaap!

With lightning speed, a line of webbing flashed down from a nearby rooftop, wrapping around the four muggers like a rope lassoing steer at a rodeo.

With a powerful tug from above, the web line pulled taut, lifting the punks off their feet, sending them rising up into the night.

Mary Jane stared up after them, stunned and searching the darkness for her rescuer. Then, one by one, the attackers came sailing down. Stepping out of the way, M.J. saw two of the punks smash through nearby windows. Another slammed into a brick wall, and the fourth crash-landed in a trash Dumpster. All lay sprawled, unconscious.

"You have a knack for getting in trouble," Spider-Man said from the shadows.

"And you have a knack for saving me," M.J. replied, walking toward him. "I think I have a superhero stalker."

Peter had not had time to put his mask on when he rushed to save M.J. It dangled from the waistband of his costume. "I was in the neighborhood," he said.

M.J. stopped, squinting at the figure in the darkness. Where had she just heard someone say that very same thing? "You are amazing," she said, stepping toward Spider-Man once more.

Fumbling with his mask, Peter finally slipped it on just as M.J. reached him. "Some people don't think so," he said.

"But you are," she replied.

"Thank you," he said, jumping onto the brick wall behind him, sticking there, feet up, head down.

M.J. stepped right up to Spider-Man. His face, though upside-down, lined up directly with hers. "Do I get to say thank you this time?" she asked, reaching for his mask and pulling it down from his chin.

Is she going to pull my mask off right here? Spider-Man wondered, unable to move to stop her.

Mary Jane stopped pulling the mask down once Spider-Man's mouth was exposed. She kissed him hard on the lips, then backed away slowly. "That's so you'll remember where your mouth is," she said softly, pulling the mask back over his chin.

Spider-Man stared at her for moment, a million thoughts racing through his head all at once. Peter Parker had finally kissed the woman he had loved his whole life, only she didn't even know it. And she wasn't kissing Peter, she was kissing Spider-Man. It was all too much to sort out. He scrambled up the brick wall, vanishing over the edge of the rooftop.

"Yowza!" Mary Jane exclaimed, exhaling deeply, staring up after him, her eyes shining in the streetlight.

CHAPTER 18

Sirens blared and thick black smoke filled the afternoon sky as a midtown apartment building burned out of control. Police cars, fire trucks, and ambulances screeched to a stop. Firefighters rushed into the building, searching for anyone who might still be trapped inside.

A few minutes later two firefighters led a frantic mother and her two young sons out of the blaze and safely across the street. The mother pulled away, desperately struggling to break free of the firefighters' grasp.

"Let me go!" she cried. "My baby is still in there! Somebody please save my baby!"

The firefighters maintained their grip. "It's too late, lady!" one said. "The roof's ready to collapse!"

"No!" the young woman shrieked, struggling unsuccessfully to break free.

Another firefighter pointed to the sky. "Look!" he shouted. "It's him!" All eyes turned skyward in time to see Spider-Man swinging toward the burning building.

"He's crazy!" the first firefighter shouted. "He hasn't got a chance!"

"Save my baby, Spider-Man!" the panicked mother pleaded. "Please!"

In a flash, Spider-Man disappeared into the blazing building—just as a large section of its roof collapsed.

"No!" screamed the grief-stricken mom, certain now that her baby was lost.

A huge fireball of orange flame and black smoke exploded from the shattered windows just below the roof. Barely inches ahead of the raging inferno, Spider-Man swooped away from the building, carrying a small parcel wrapped in protective webbing.

"I don't believe it!" a firefighter yelled. "He's alive, and he's got the kid!"

The crowd that had gathered broke into spontaneous applause as Spider-Man landed beside the young mom. "Here's your baby," he said, handing over the web-wrapped bundle.

"Oh, bless you, Spider-Man," the weeping mom said, tears of joy streaming down her cheeks. She peeled the soft web blanket away and kissed her baby on the forehead. "Thank you!"

"Now, you boys be good," Spider-Man said sternly, turning to the baby's two older brothers. "Never play with matches!"

"Help me!" came a horrified shriek from the burning building.

"Look!" a young man in the crowd shouted, pointing to a window on a lower floor. "There's someone else in there!"

The crowd turned back toward the building and spotted an older woman standing in the window, wrapped in a shawl, waving her hands and screaming frantically.

Leaping into the air, Spider-Man fired a web strand and swung back toward the flaming structure. Flipping through an adjacent window, he landed in a smoke-filled room and saw the terrified woman huddled in a corner, her shawl pulled tightly around her.

"Everything's going to be okay, ma'am," Spider-Man announced. "I'll get you out of here."

"Oh, thank you, sonny," the old woman said weakly. "You're my hero!" Standing up, the woman cast off her shawl to reveal that she was, in fact, the Green Goblin!

"What's wrong with lighting up now and then?" The Green Goblin cackled, straightening up to his full height, surrounded by approaching flames.

"Green Goblin!" Spider-Man cried. "You started this fire!"

"You're so pathetically predictable, web-head," the Green Goblin taunted. "Like a moth to flame. I just knew you'd show up. So, what about my proposal to join forces? Are you in or out?"

"It's you who's out, Gobby," Spider-Man replied, closing his fists, preparing for battle. "Out for good!"

But before Spider-Man could move, the Green Goblin flung a razor bat right at him. Spider-Man reacted instinctively, deflecting the sharp spinning blade with his right arm, but the finely honed weapon sliced a deep gash in his forearm.

"Ahhh!" Spider-Man cried, clutching his throbbing right arm in his left hand. Looking down, he saw a large wound dripping blood. He quickly fired a web strand up to a burning beam above the Green Goblin's head. Yanking hard on the webbing, Spider-Man pulled the beam down onto the Green Goblin.

But the Green Goblin was fast and strong. He hoisted the flaming beam off and turned to confront Spider-Man—but he was gone, disappeared out the window, trailing blood behind him.

"I don't forgive and I don't forget, Spider-Man!" the Green Goblin howled fiercely, climbing onto his glider, preparing to fly from the blaze. "You can consider my offer of a partnership withdrawn!"

Thanksgiving was always Peter's favorite holiday. Each year he looked forward to Aunt May's great cooking, watching a little football with Uncle Ben, and the warm, loving family feeling that was especially evident in their home at holiday times.

This year, with the loss of Uncle Ben, everything seemed wrong. Peter wondered how he and Aunt May would get through this first celebration without him. He almost felt like not celebrating at all.

Peter was greatly relieved when Harry and Mary Jane suggested that they all celebrate this year at Harry and Peter's apartment in the city. Peter, Aunt May, Harry, and Mary Jane would also be joined by Norman Osborn. Aunt May would still get to make her famous turkey, Norman would finally get to meet Mary Jane, and the pain of Uncle Ben's absence would be eased slightly by the pleasure of celebrating with a group of close friends and family.

As Aunt May pulled the sizzling turkey from the oven, poking it with a fork, Mary Jane checked on the sweet potatoes. Harry finished setting the dining room table for five. There was still no sign of Norman or Peter.

The doorbell rang and Harry jumped nervously. "Okay," he called into the kitchen. "He's here!"

Mary Jane came scurrying out of the kitchen, untying her apron and tossing it back onto the kitchen counter, revealing a stylish black dress.

"You look great!" Harry said, walking quickly to the door. "That dress is beautiful!"

M.J. smiled nervously. The man she was about to meet was not only her boyfriend's father, but the great Norman Osborn, captain of industry, a genuine big shot.

Harry opened the door and Norman stepped in, dressed impeccably in a dark suit. He carried a bakery box tied with string.

"Sorry I'm late. Work was murder," Norman said, quickly handing the box to Harry, then looking right at Mary Jane. "Here's a fruitcake. Who's this young lady?"

"M.J.," Harry began, taking a deep breath. "I'd like you to meet my father, Norman Osborn. Dad, I'd like you to meet Mary Jane Watson, M.J."

Mary Jane flashed a radiant smile that lit up her beautiful face, framed by shimmering copper-colored hair. Norman stepped over to her, extending his right hand, all the while studying this young woman who had lately occupied so much of his son's time and attention.

"How do you do?" he said softly. "I've been looking forward to meeting you."

"Happy Thanksgiving, sir," M.J. responded, grasping and shaking his hand. An unexplainable feeling of dread came over her. She shook it off as Aunt May came in from the kitchen.

"Hello, Norman," Aunt May said warmly, wiping her hands on her apron. "We're so pleased you're here. Well, that just leaves Peter. I wonder where he is. He better have remembered the cranberry sauce."

At that moment, a blue-and-red streak flashed past the dining room window, unnoticed by everyone in the room. Peter, still in his costume, slipped through his bedroom window, landing on the floor with a thud.

Everyone in the living room turned toward Peter's bedroom door. "That's weird," Harry said. "I didn't think Peter was here."

In his bedroom Peter yanked off his mask, then looked down at the gash on his arm. A knock came suddenly at his door. "Pete?" called Harry. "You in there?"

The door swung open and Harry, Aunt May, and Norman stepped in. The room was empty. "There's nobody here," Aunt May said. "Now that's odd."

Clinging to his bedroom ceiling, Peter held his breath and looked down at the trio in the room. Harry and Aunt May walked back out the door as Norman lingered for a moment. As he turned to leave, a single drop of blood from Peter's wound fell, landing onto the carpet.

Norman's enhanced sense of hearing picked up the almost imperceptible sound, and he spun around, spotting the glob of red spreading through the carpet. He glanced up quickly and found himself looking at a blank ceiling. Rushing to the window, he searched in all directions, but saw no one. Shrugging, he returned to the dining room.

Peter clung below the window ledge, motionless. When Norman had left the room, he slipped back in, changed into street clothes, and scrambled back out the window. A few seconds later, he let himself in the front door.

"Hey, everyone!" he shouted, pulling a small brown paper bag from his jacket pocket. "Sorry I took so long. It's a jungle out there. I had to hit a little old lady with a stick to get these cranberries."

Aunt May shook her head and rolled her eyes at Peter's joke. Kids! "Come on, everyone," she announced. "Let's sit down and say a prayer."

As everyone took their seats, Aunt May noticed blood on Peter's arm. "Peter, you're bleeding!" she cried.

"I stepped off a curb and got clipped by a bike messenger," Peter said, having come up with his story only a moment earlier.

"Well, let me see," Aunt May said, standing up and taking Peter's arm into her hands. She pushed his sleeve up, revealing the X-shaped wound. "What in heaven's name? I'll get the first-aid kit and clean that up. And then we'll say grace. This is the boys' first Thanksgiving in their own apartment and we're going to do things properly."

As Aunt May walked from the table, Norman stared at Peter's cut. He eyes opened wide with recognition at the sight of the familiar X-shaped gash.

"How did you say that happened?" Norman asked, eyeing Peter suspiciously.

"Bike messenger knocked me down," he replied, just as his spider sense went wild. His whole body tingled like crazy, his brain flashing a nonstop warning. But why? He glanced around the room. Who here could pose a threat?

Norman stood up abruptly, stunned by the only possible

explanation for Peter's distinctive wound. "You'll have to excuse me," he said, walking toward the door. "I'm afraid I have to go."

Harry leaped from his seat and raced after his father. "What?" he cried. "Why?"

"Something has come to my attention," Norman replied, sweat breaking out on his forehead, his heart pounding.

"Are you all right, Dad?" Harry asked, overwhelmed with anger and confusion.

"I'm fine," he said curtly to Harry. Then he looked at Aunt May, who had just returned with the first-aid kit. "Thank you, Aunt May. Good-bye, everyone."

"Oh, dear," Aunt May cried. "What happened?"

Norman looked at Peter, his eyes narrowing. Then he stepped out of the apartment.

"Dad!" Harry shouted, chasing him down the hallway, leaving the apartment door open behind him. "What are you doing? I planned this whole thing so that you could meet M.J. and you barely even looked at her!"

Norman leaned against the hallway wall, his mind racing. "I've got to go."

Harry grabbed his father by the shoulders, trembling as he spoke. "Hey, I like this girl, Dad!" he shouted. "This is impor-tant to me!"

"Harry, please," Norman began, straightening up, switching to the tone of voice he used when he needed to let Harry know exactly who was in charge. "Look at that girl. You think she's sniffing around you because she likes your person-ality?"

"What are you saying, Dad?" Harry asked in shock. His

father had said some nasty things to him before, but this took the cake!

"She's just after your money," Norman snarled. Then he turned and headed down the stairs to the street.

"What!" Harry shouted to his father's retreating back. It was too late. Norman was gone.

When Harry returned to the apartment, M.J. was grabbing her coat. "Where are you going?' he asked as she headed for the door.

"Thanks for sticking up for me, Harry," she said, pushing past him.

"You heard?" Harry asked, embarrassed.

"Everyone could hear that creep!" Mary Jane shouted.

Harry's face reddened with anger. "That 'creep' is my father!" he shouted. "If I'm lucky I'll become half of what he is. So just keep your mouth shut about things you don't understand."

"Harry Osborn!" Aunt May cried, reprimanding him.

"You're acting like somebody's father," M.J. yelled at Harry. "Like mine!" Reaching the door, she looked over her shoulder. "I'm sorry, Aunt May," she said, fighting back the tears. Then she left, slamming the door behind her.

"Harry, go after her!" Peter shouted at his roommate, pointing at the door.

"I don't think so," Harry replied coldly, shaking his head.

"Come on, Harry, go!" Peter repeated.

"No, I can't," he said. Then turning to Aunt May he added, "Welcome to an Osborn Thanksgiving." He stormed into his bedroom, slamming the door shut.

116

Peter turned and kissed his aunt on the cheek. "Sorry, Aunt May," he said rushing out of the apartment. "Everything looked great!"

The apartment door closed behind Peter. Aunt May sat alone at the beautiful table they had all worked so hard to create. This was going to be different. Difficult, yes, without her beloved Ben, but still a joyful family gathering. Now everything was wrong.

Steam still wafted from the uncarved turkey. The candles flickered elegantly in the dim light. Aunt May shook her head and sighed.

"We didn't even get to say grace," she said sadly.

CHAPTER 19

Peter raced from the building and found Mary Jane sitting on the front steps of a nearby apartment house. She was crying, her eye makeup dripping down her cheeks in black streaks. Peter sat down beside her, handing her a handkerchief.

"I'm sorry I acted like that," M.J. said, wiping the tears, then blowing her nose. "I just couldn't stay there. Being treated like that brings back too much bad stuff."

"I understand," Peter said. "I've never seen Harry or Mr. Osborn act like that before. But I do know Harry really loves you."

"Sometimes I wonder why I went out with him in the first place," M.J. said, shaking her head. "I guess it's because he asked me. He said I looked great in this dress. Thought it would impress his father. That's a laugh!"

"Well, you do look extremely beautiful in it," Peter said, before he had a chance to think about what he was saying.

M.J. looked right at him and smiled warmly. "Thank you," she replied, putting her arm around his shoulder. "You look very handsome yourself tonight."

Their eyes met. Peter had never felt more in love with M.J. His big chance was at hand. He looked away. Another opportunity wasted.

Norman Osborn knelt on the floor of his study, staring down at the Green Goblin mask he clutched in his hands. The room was dark except for a small pool of light cast by a desk lamp, illuminating Norman and the mask.

The mask spoke to him, though it didn't move. Its voice rang in Norman's head as if the Green Goblin were standing next to him in the room.

"This changes everything," the mask said. "Spider-Man is all but invincible. But Peter Parker is simply flesh and blood. We must destroy Parker. Then we'll be rid of Spider-Man."

"I can't!" Norman cried, replying to the mask. "I've been like a father to that boy. He's been like my *good* son."

"He came to you, Norman," the mask continued, "a greedy, scheming orphan who plucked your heartstrings, worming his way in, leaving no room for Harry, your true son and heir!"

Norman stared at the mask in shock. "He did!" Norman exclaimed. "It's true. What have I done to Harry, my own son?"

"After everything you've done for Parker, look how he repays you," the mask went on, the voice filling Norman's head. "He fights you as Spider-Man."

"What can I do?" Norman asked weakly.

"Teach him about loss and pain," the mask replied. "Make him wish he was dead, and then grant that wish."

"Yes," Norman said, his mouth turning up into a twisted smile. "But how?"

"The cunning warrior attacks neither body nor mind," the mask said. "The heart, Norman. First we attack the heart!"

Aunt May missed her husband terribly. With Peter living on his own, the house felt so big and empty. Nights were the toughest. It was easy enough to keep busy during the day, to keep her mind occupied, to spend time with friends. But as each day drew to a close, the ache grew more acute, and the hole in her life left by Uncle Ben's death seemed to grow bigger with the passage of time.

She slipped on her flannel pajamas, then kissed the picture of Ben on her nightstand. Lowering herself to the floor, her knees aching, she knelt beside her bed and prayed.

"Our Father, who art in heaven, hallowed be thy name," she began, hands together, elbows resting on the bed. "Thy kingdom come, thy will be done, on Earth as it is in Heaven. Give us this day our daily bread, and forgive us our trespasses, as we forgive those who trespass against us. Lead us not into temptation, but—"

Without warning, the wall behind Aunt May exploded, spraying glass and plaster all over the bedroom. Aunt May fell to the floor, where she lay trembling.

Looking up, she saw the Green Goblin hovering over her on his glider. A thin stream of sickly green gas rushed from the glider, filling the room with a toxic haze.

"Finish it!" the Green Goblin demanded, his unearthly

yellow eyes staring right at Aunt May. She felt as if they would burn right through her. "Finish it!"

"D-Deliver us from evil!" she stammered, pleading. Then she passed out, overcome by the gas.

"Amen, sister!" the Green Goblin cackled, his hideous laugh filling the house and spilling out onto the quiet Queens street.

Peter frantically raced down the hospital corridor, panic and fear driving him, blocking out all thoughts except one—*find Aunt May*. Reaching her room, he skidded to a stop.

As he stepped in, Peter saw doctors and nurses hovering around the bed. He pushed his way through the crowd to her bedside. Aunt May lay sleeping, hooked up to several rapidly beeping machines, tubes extending from her nose, IVs running down into her arm.

"Aunt May!" he cried. Turning to a doctor, he asked, "What happened? Is she going to be okay?"

"Sir, please," a nurse replied, taking Peter's arm and leading him to the door. "Let the doctors work!"

Just before he left the room, Peter heard Aunt May moan. He turned to look back at her in time to hear her mutter weakly. "Those eyes," she gasped. "Those horrible yellow eyes!" Then a doctor covered her mouth with an oxygen mask.

Peter stepped into the hall. The door to Aunt May's room closed behind him. His eyes widened in terror as the meaning of Aunt May's words became clear. "The Green Goblin," he mumbled. "He knows who I am! But how? How could he know!"

His mind racing, unable to sit still in the hospital waiting room, Peter left, stepping out into the chilled night air and walking quickly. He realized that without even thinking about it, he was heading toward Aunt May's house, the place he still thought of as home.

At the house he picked up a few things he thought Aunt May might need. He tossed these into a bag and headed back to the hospital.

This time when he entered the room, all was quiet. Aunt May was alone, sleeping peacefully, the machines surrounding her beeping more slowly, steadily. Peter emptied the bag, placing Aunt May's hairbrush, pajamas, and a few other things into the drawers of the night table beside her bed. He placed a favorite framed photo of himself with Aunt May and Uncle Ben on top of the night table, near Aunt May's head.

Lowering himself slowly into a bedside chair, Peter gently took Aunt May's hand into his. "I'm sorry," he said, staring at the photo, thinking about Uncle Ben's death and Aunt May nearly suffering the same fate, all because of him and his life as Spider-Man. "I'm so sorry." He leaned down and kissed her forehead, blinking back tears.

The following afternoon Mary Jane made her way down the hospital hallway carrying a large bouquet of flowers. Finding the correct room, she peeked inside and saw Peter, still seated in the chair. He had a science textbook open in his lap. Various fast-food bags and empty coffee cups were scattered around the room. M.J. smiled, then gently tapped on the door. Peter looked up.

"Okay if I come in?" she asked.

He nodded. M.J. walked to his side and put her arms around his neck, hugging him tightly.

"I'm so sorry," she said placing the flowers on the bedside table, then leaning over and softly touching Aunt May's forehead. "Will she be okay?"

"We think so," Peter sighed, the strain of this ordeal and his bedside vigil clearly showing in his voice. "She finally woke up this morning for a while. Thanks for coming."

"Who would do this to her?" M.J. asked incredulously. "Your aunt May is so loving, so giving. Who would want to hurt her?"

"The Green Goblin," Peter explained, choking up as he spoke.

"But why?" M.J. asked, even more shocked. "Why would he need to hurt her? I'm sorry, Peter. You must be asking yourself all these same questions."

"It's okay," he replied, looking up at M.J.'s face. "How about you? Are you all right about the other night?"

"I'm sorry about that," M.J. said, shaking her head. "It just makes things worse for everybody."

"You certainly have a right to be upset," Peter said softly. "Have you called Harry?"

"He called me but I haven't called him back," M.J. answered, turning away from Peter. "The fact is, I'm in love with someone else."

"You are?" Peter said, his heart pounding wildly. Could it be?

"At least I think I am," M.J. said. "It's funny. He's saved my life twice and I've never seen his face."

"Oh, him," Peter said, secretly pleased, but also a little disappointed at the same time. "He *is* extremely cool."

"Do you think those terrible things they say about him are true?" M.J. asked.

"No way," Peter replied. "I know him a little. I'm sort of his unofficial photographer. And none of that stuff is true."

"How do you always manage to find him?" M.J. asked.

"Wrong place, right time, I guess," Peter said, shrugging.

"Do you ever talk to him?" M.J. asked.

"Sometimes," Peter said.

"Does he ever talk about me?" M.J. asked.

"Um-uh, yeah," Peter stammered. "Once he asked me what I thought of you."

"Really?" M.J. said, surprised. "And what did you say?.

"I told him," Peter began. "I said, 'Spidey'—I call him Spidey sometimes—'the thing about M.J. is, when you look in her eyes and she's looking back at yours and smiling, you feel stronger and weaker at the same time. You feel both excited and terrified. And you know the kind of man you want to be. When you're with her, it's as if you've reached the unreachable, and you weren't ready for it.'"

Peter looked and up saw the tears welling in M.J.'s eyes.

"You said that?" she asked softly.

"Uh, something like that, yeah," Peter replied.

Neither Peter nor Mary Jane noticed Aunt May awakening. M.J. reached out and squeezed Peter's hand. Their eyes met and she took a step toward him.

That's when Harry walked into the room, carrying a bouquet for Aunt May. "Hello," he said, as all three felt a flush of embarrassment.

M.J. quickly dropped Peter's hand. Harry stared at both of them coldly.

"I've got to go," Harry said, handing Peter the flowers. "I hope Aunt May is all right." Then he turned and raced from the room.

CHAPTER 20

Harry walked briskly down the street, his hands shoved deeply into his pockets, shoulders bent, eyes focused on the few feet of sidewalk in front of him. He loved Mary Jane and regretted the Thanksgiving Day incident. He had hoped they could patch things up. But then to walk in on M.J. and Peter holding hands, looking at each other that way. What was he to do now?

Entering the building in which his father lived, Harry let himself into Norman's apartment. "Dad?" he called out.

He got no answer, but saw a light on upstairs. When he reached the bottom of the staircase, he heard voices from the upstairs study—two voices, he thought, though he wasn't sure.

"What is it?' Norman yelled down, quickly walking to the top of the stairs.

Harry stopped at the base of the staircase. "You were right about M.J., Dad," Harry said, looking up at his father who was hidden in shadow. "She's in love with Peter."

"Parker?" Norman said, starting slowly down the stairs. "And how does he feel about her?"

"Are you kidding?" Harry answered quickly with a smirk. "Peter's been in love with her since the fourth grade."

A sly smile spread across Norman's face. Now, this was a piece of information he—they—could use. Norman wiped the smile from his face as he reached the bottom of the stairs. "I'm sorry," he said grasping Harry's shoulder firmly. "I know I haven't always been there for you, Harry."

Harry was caught off guard. On top of everything else, he was not quite ready to delve into his feelings toward his father. "You're busy," he said, shrugging, as if all the missed appointments, broken promises, and high-pressure expectations could be wiped away with the gesture. "You're an important man. I understand that."

"That's no excuse," Norman said, putting his arm around Harry's shoulder. "I'm proud of you, Harry. Proud that you're my son. I'm going to make it up to you. I promise."

Then Norman did something he hadn't done in years. He reached out with both arms and hugged Harry.

The hug was nice, Harry thought, yet there was something very creepy about it.

That evening in Aunt May's hospital room, Peter sat in the bedside chair, a notebook open on his lap, a pencil in his hands, and his eyes shut. He was sound asleep. Waking with a jolt from a bizarre dream, he looked around, yawned, and rubbed his eyes with the back of his hand.

"Peter," Aunt May said weakly.

"Huh?" Peter moaned, still trying to focus. "Oh, Aunt May, you're awake. That's great. You're okay."

"I'm okay," Aunt May said. "But I think *you* should go home and get some sleep."

"I don't like to leave you," he replied.

"I'm safe here," Aunt May said, smiling.

"I should have been there, Aunt May," Peter said, the guilt rushing up from his stomach, getting caught in his throat. "Maybe I could have done something."

Aunt May chuckled softly at the thought of her Peter—the book-loving science student—playing the role of hero. "You do too much already," she said. "College, a job, all this time with me. You're not Superman, you know!"

Peter laughed. If she only knew just how funny that was.

"Well, a smile on your face," Aunt May said, perking up. "I haven't seen one of those since Mary Jane was here."

Peter gave her a look of comically exaggerated annoyance. "Hey!" he said, pretending outrage, but really feeling a little embarrassed. "You were *supposed* to be asleep! What did you hear?"

Ignoring the question, Aunt May closed her eyes slightly as her mind drifted back in time. "When you were six years old," she began, "M.J.'s family moved in next door. The first time you saw her, you said, 'Aunt May, is that an angel?'"

"Did I really say that?" Peter asked, having no recollection of the day.

"You sure did," Aunt May replied. "She'd like to know that, don't you think?"

"Harry's in love with her," Peter explained. "She's still his girl."

"Isn't that up to her?' Aunt May asked.

"She doesn't really know me," Peter said, voicing the excuse he had used on himself for years.

"Because you won't let her get to know you," Aunt May replied, not buying the excuse for a second. "You're so mysterious all the time, even more so lately. Don't be so complicated. And don't let any more time go by. Tell me, Peter. Would it be so dangerous to let Mary Jane know how much you care? It's not as if everyone doesn't already know you love her."

Dangerous? The word sounded an instant alarm in Peter's brain. Dangerous, yes, but not in the way Aunt May meant.

"Thanks, Aunt May," Peter said, getting up and kissing her cheek. "I need to think about all this. I'll be back soon. I'm glad you're feeling better."

Peter walked swiftly to a pay phone in the hospital corridor. Dropping a quarter into the slot, he dialed quickly, then waited. One ring, then two, then a third.

"Answer the phone," he grumbled anxiously into the receiver. "Answer it!"

M.J.'s answering machine picked up. "Hi, it's me. Sing your song at the beep." *Beeeeep.*

"M.J., it's Peter, are you there?" he began, trying not to let his concern show. "Just checking to make sure you're safe and sound. You know, I'm worried about you. Give me a call, I'll give you an update on Aunt May. Hey, where are you? How come you're not there? Okay, take care. Don't go up any dark alleys."

Just as Peter was about to hang up, he heard someone pick up the phone on the other end. "Oh, great! You're there!" he said. "Hello? M.J.?"

Instead of M.J.'s sweet voice, Peter heard a strange sound coming through the phone. As the sound grew louder Peter recognized it and froze with fear. There was no mistaking the repulsive cackle of the Green Goblin.

"Can Spider-Man come out and play?" the Green Goblin asked in a mocking sing-song voice.

"Where is she?" Peter demanded angrily.

"Be of love a little more careful, Spider-Man," the Green Goblin recited. Then he let loose a sickening giggle and hung up the phone.

CHAPTER 21

Mary Jane slowly opened her eyes, awakening as if from a long sleep. In truth she had been unconscious for less than an hour, the latest victim of the Green Goblin's powerful hallucinogenic gas. As her mind cleared and her vision focused, she pulled herself up to her feet, clutching her aching head. Taking a step backward, she felt her balance tipping. Windmilling her arms to regain her footing, she grabbed the steel girder beside her and stopped herself from falling.

Looking down, she spotted cars zooming back and forth along a roadway—the roadway of a bridge hundreds of feet below her. She recognized the bridge, having driven across it about a million times. The fog lifted from her brain, replaced by sheer terror, as Mary Jane realized that she now stood atop the western tower of the Queensboro Bridge!

"Don't panic! Don't panic! Don't panic!" M.J. repeated to herself as panic set in. She heard a high-pitched whine and turned just in time to see the Green Goblin zoom overhead on his glider, heading for the Roosevelt Island tram station.

The bright red tram carried passengers from Manhattan

over to Roosevelt Island, a small residential island in the middle of the East River, halfway between Manhattan and Queens. The tram itself rode up and over the river on a cable that ran alongside the bridge. At the moment the tram was full of eight-year-olds and their parents, returning home from a school outing.

A blurry flash of movement streaked past the bridge and came to rest on a nearby building. Spider-Man had been out searching for the Green Goblin and M.J. It was now obvious to him that the Green Goblin wanted to be found, having picked such a public place to stage his final showdown with the Webbed Wonder.

Spider-Man quickly surveyed the scene—the Green Goblin flying toward the tram station, M.J. trapped on the bridge tower, the crowded tram slowly making its way over the river. This added up to trouble—big trouble!

As the Green Goblin approached the tram station, a rocket launcher emerged from the bottom of the glider. With a mere movement of his arm, the Green Goblin fired a rocket right at the station.

Fooom!

The tram station exploded in a massive inferno of orange flames and black smoke, lighting up the night, sending chunks of flaming debris soaring into the air.

Searing chunks of the tram station rained down on the bridge roadway, sending cars slamming into each other, spinning out of control, trying to avoid the hurtling wreckage. Above the river, the tram rocked back and forth as its support cable shook from the impact of the blast. The kids on board shrieked in terror.

Spider-Man fired a web strand and swung across the river, landing on the bridge.

Snap! Whip!

The tram's support cable snapped with a sickening sound, sending the car full of children and their parents plunging toward the river below.

With an incredible burst of speed and an amazing display of strength, the Green Goblin rocketed toward the plummeting tram, snatching its cable in mid-air. The cable pulled taut, held fast in the Green Goblin's powerful grip. The tram car bounced and shook to a halt high above the churning river.

The Green Goblin's glider stopped right in front of Mary Jane. Leaping from the hovering glider, the Green Goblin landed on the bridge tower. Never losing his grasp on the cable, he grabbed Mary Jane with his free hand, dangling her helplessly above the roadway.

"Spider-Man!" the Green Goblin shouted up to the blue-and-red–clad figure who hung, frozen, from the bridge. "This is why only fools are heroes! Because you never know when someone will come along with a sadistic choice!"

Spider-Man looked from Mary Jane to the tram, then back again. He was paralyzed. The Green Goblin had set him up in a no-win situation. No matter what he did, someone would die.

"What's it going to be, hero?" the Green Goblin shouted. "Let die the woman you love?" He extended his arm, pushing Mary Jane further out over the gathering crowd and the jumble of cars below.

"Or suffer the little children?" he cackled, releasing his grip on the tram cable for a moment. The cable slipped through his fist. The tram dropped rapidly, before the Green Goblin tightened his grip again, causing the car to stop suddenly, sending the passengers tumbling to its floor.

"Make your choice, Spider-Man," he demanded. "And see how a hero is rewarded. This is your doing. You have caused this. This is the life you have chosen. Now, choose!"

With that, the Green Goblin released both the cable and Mary Jane.

Spider-Man leaped from his perch on the bridge, catching M.J. around the waist with one arm, firing a web strand back up at the bridge with the other.

"Hold on!" he shouted, swinging down toward the plunging tram, releasing his web and using the free hand to grab the tram's cable. Shifting Mary Jane onto his back, he fired another web line from his newly freed wrist.

The web line stuck to the bottom of the bridge, pulling taut. The tram car bounced wildly. Spider-Man felt as if his body would rip in two. His right hand clutched his web line, the other end of which was secured to the bridge. His left hand held the tram cable, his muscles straining to support its enormous weight. On his back, Mary Jane held on tightly for dear life.

"Climb down," Spider-Man shouted over his shoulder. Mary Jane looked at him, confused. "Climb down the cable to the tram!"

"I can't!" she cried, her voice quivering. "I'm scared."

"M.J., just do it!" Spider-Man pleaded. "Trust me!"

M.J. nodded, then began the slow climb, slipping off Spider-Man's back, then lowering herself down the thin metal cable.

When M.J. was halfway down the cable, Spider-Man heard the all-too-familiar whine of the Green Goblin's glider behind him. Turning his head, Spider-Man was struck by the full force of the Green Goblin's fist. The powerful blow sent him swaying back and forth. He struggled now not only to maintain his grip on the cable, but to remain conscious as well.

M.J. dangled from the cable beneath Spider-Man's feet, as the tram car below her rocked and spun, sending the people inside banging into the car's walls.

The Green Goblin swung his glider in a wide arc, circling back for another pass at Spider-Man. He cackled maniacally, as he closed in on the helpless hero. Extending his arm, the Green Goblin sliced at Spider-Man's mid-section with a razor-sharp blade, sending blood-spattered bits of Spider-Man's costume fluttering to the river below.

The impact of the Green Goblin's blow caused Spider-Man to lose his grip on the tram cable. It zipped through his open hand. With pain searing his body, Spider-Man lunged for the end of the cable, grabbing it just as it passed his feet, stopping the tram's plunge once more.

This time, the jolt of the cable going taut tossed Mary Jane off. She fell, landing hard on the top of the tram.

With an evil grin and the intention of finishing off his enemy, the Green Goblin raced toward Spider-Man, his glider at full throttle.

Spider-Man braced for the impact, not sure he could handle another blow. The Green Goblin approached, drawing back his fist, when suddenly a huge chunk of asphalt struck him in the side of the head. He spiraled out of control, spinning right past Spider-Man.

As the Green Goblin struggled to right his glider, the barrage continued from below. Down on the bridge's roadway, the crowd of New Yorkers was grabbing and throwing anything they could get their hands on, from chunks of the roadway, to bottles and hubcaps.

"Ahhh!" the Green Goblin shrieked, covering his head with his hands, flying away from the shower of debris.

Looking down at the cheering crowd, Spider-Man felt a burst of renewed energy. It didn't matter what the papers said. These were real New Yorkers. Nobody told them what to think. And right now, based on the evidence before their eyes, they unanimously thought that Spider-Man was a hero.

Spider-Man spied a massive mound of rock extending from the bridge's support piling. He wasn't positive that it would be big enough to hold the tram, but he didn't have many other options. Slowly, he began to lower the tram—with M.J. on its roof—to the large rock below.

After a few tense moments, the tram touched down on the rock and came to rest. Mary Jane stood up on its roof and smiled adoringly up at Spider-Man, who took a deep breath of relief.

From out of nowhere, a rope wrapped around Spider-Man's waist. The Green Goblin— recovered from the crowd's attack—held tightly onto the other end of the rope, then zoomed away, pulling Spider-Man along behind his glider.

The crowd on the bridge let out a collective gasp, while Mary Jane looked on in horror at this latest assault.

As the glider approached Roosevelt Island, the Green Goblin sliced through the rope with his blade, cutting Spider-Man loose. Spider-Man plummeted, crashing into the hulking ruin of an abandoned hospital on the island below.

Roaring down to the ruin, the Green Goblin landed his glider, leaped off, and stood over Spider-Man, relishing his apparent victory. "I tried to make my case to you, but you just wouldn't listen," the Green Goblin said, mock sympathy dripping from his voice. "Your sweetheart's death would have been quick and painless. Now it will be slow and torturous."

Reaching back into the glider, the Green Goblin pulled out a long rod. Pressing a button on the rod, three sharp blades popped out, forming a deadly pitchfork. "Slow and torturous," he repeated. "Just like yours!"

The Green Goblin aimed his weapon at Spider-Man's heart, then brought it down with a savage thrust. Just before it struck his chest, Spider-Man reached up and grabbed the weapon, yanking it from the Green Goblin's hands.

Spider-Man sat up, then slammed the rod into the Green Goblin's head, sending him flying across the ruin. He landed in a pile of rubble. Spider-Man leaped to his feet, snapped the rod in two across his knee, and tossed the pieces aside.

The fury boiling up inside him filled Spider-Man with renewed strength. He grabbed the Green Goblin, lifting him off the ground, then delivered a devastating blow to his jaw. The Green Goblin crashed into the remains of a stone wall, then crumpled to the ground in a pitiful heap.

"Please," he moaned, as Spider-Man pulled his fist back for the final punch of this drawn-out contest. "Peter, please." The Green Goblin pulled off his mask and Spider-Man found himself staring into the face of Norman Osborn.

"It can't be!" Spider-Man cried, dropping his fist. "You're a

137

monster. You killed those people on the balcony. You could have killed your own son up there. You tried to kill Aunt May and Mary Jane!"

"Not me!" Osborn whimpered. "I'm not a monster. *It* killed those people. The Green Goblin did it. I had nothing to do with it. Please, don't let it have me again. Don't let it take me back!"

Spider-Man stared at Osborn, trying to understand the terrible evil that had taken over this man he had once respected. As he cowered and begged, Osborn secretly pressed a button on the control panel of his costume.

Slowly, silently, the Green Goblin rose into the air behind Peter, a sharp spear extending from its front.

"Give me your hand, Peter," Osborn pleaded, getting to his feet and reaching out with his right hand. "Believe in me as I believed in you. I was like a father to you. Be a son to me now."

Spider-Man stepped back, refusing Osborn's hand. "I had a father," he said sternly. "His name was Ben Parker."

Norman Osborn began to laugh, his cackle rising in pitch and volume. At that moment Spider-Man's spider sense went off. His head tingled and the feeling that something was behind him overwhelmed his entire being.

Spinning around, he saw the Green Goblin racing right toward him. Diving out of the way, he somersaulted, then sprang to his feet just in time to see the glider's spear pass right through Norman Osborn, pinning him to a wall.

Osborn slumped over, dead, blood pouring from his Green Goblin costume.

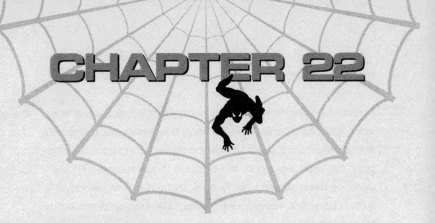

CHAPTER 22

The police arrived at the Queensboro Bridge, and soon the passengers and Mary Jane were evacuated safely from the tram.

Spider-Man carried the dead body of Norman Osborn back to Osborn's apartment. Landing on a small balcony, he entered the apartment through two large French doors.

Removing the Green Goblin costume, Spider-Man dressed Norman in his own clothes. Blood soaked through Osborn's shirt.

As Spidey placed the limp body gently onto the floor, the door to the apartment swung open and Harry walked in.

"You!" Harry shouted at the sight of Spider-Man standing over his father's lifeless body and blood-soaked shirt. "You're a murderer!"

"No," Spider-Man replied, raising his hands and shaking his head. "It's not what it looks like!"

"Murderer!" Harry screamed again, racing to a nearby table, opening a drawer, and pulling out a gun. He turned back toward Spider-Man, but Spider-Man was gone, vanished back out into the New York night.

The curtains on the open French doors flapped in the breeze as Harry knelt down beside his father and wept.

Norman Osborn's funeral was well attended. Business leaders and military brass were among the mourners, along with friends and family. Aunt May, recently released from the hospital, felt well enough to attend. She stood talking with Mary Jane as Peter walked Harry back to the Osborn Bentley.

"I'm so sorry, Harry," Peter said. "I know what it's like to lose a father."

"I didn't lose him," Harry replied angrily. "He was stolen from me. And I swear on my father's grave that one day Spider-Man will pay!"

Peter remained tight-lipped, thinking about his best friend, who had now become Spider-Man's worst enemy.

When they reached the car, Harry looked Peter right in the eyes. "Look, about M.J.," he began. "I was just trying to impress my dad by going out with a beautiful woman. I knew she was never right for me. I'm just so thankful that you're my friend. You're all the family I have left."

Harry hugged Peter warmly, then slipped into the Bentley and slowly drove away.

Peter walked through the cemetery, alone with his thoughts. *Why is it that no matter what I do, no matter how hard I try, the people I love the most are always the ones who pay?*

He stopped at a grave and looked down at the headstone. It read: BEN PARKER, BELOVED HUSBAND AND UNCLE.

"Hey!" called a voice from behind him. It was M.J. "Your aunt thought I'd find you here."

"M.J.'s here, Uncle Ben," Peter said, looking down at the headstone.

"You must miss him so much," M.J. said, stepping up beside Peter.

"He was a beautiful guy," Peter replied.

They turned and left the grave, walking silently for a while. Mary Jane finally broke the silence.

"There's something I've been wanting to tell you," she said. "I heard the message you left on my answering machine. You didn't finish, but I know what you wanted to say. Only now, I want to say it first.

"When I was up on the bridge and I thought I was going to die, there was only one person I was thinking of, and it's not who you think it is. It was you. I thought, I just want to see Peter Parker's face one more time."

"My face?" Peter said in amazement.

"I've been so stupid for so long," M.J. continued. "There's only one man who was always there for me, who makes me believe that I'm more than I ever thought I was, that knows I'm just me, but it's okay. The truth is, I love you, Peter!"

Peter could not believe that this was actually happening. M.J. standing here telling him that she loves him. But he couldn't tell her how he felt. He couldn't, not as long as he was Spider-Man. He had learned his lesson. Can't get too close. People he loved got hurt, and he was never going to let that happen again.

"I can't tell you everything," Peter blurted out. "I mean, there's so much to tell. To tell you, the girl next door."

"But is that all I am?" Mary Jane asked.

"Oh, no," Peter replied. "You're the amazing girl next door.

141

And I will always be there to take care of you. I wish I could give you more than that, but you must know that you will always be safe."

Mary Jane looked up at Peter, then closed her eyes and kissed him, a long magical kiss. She had experienced a kiss like this only once before, the time she kissed Spider-Man. But this one was every bit as wonderful.

I can't give her what she wants, Peter thought when their lips had separated. *I can't*. With the warm glow of love still on Mary Jane's face, Peter turned and walked away, struggling with his decision.

Then Uncle Ben's voice came to him, and he understood that he had made the right choice, the only choice to make sure that no one ever again hurt the people he loved.

"Remember," Uncle Ben said. "With great power comes great responsibility."

Peter Parker would never, ever, forget those words again.

EPILOGUE

J. Jonah Jameson slammed the latest edition of the *Daily Bugle* down onto his desk. A bunch of freshly cut flowers on the desk shook in their vase.

"Spider-Man!" he blustered at Robbie Robertson. "I just don't get it. First the town thinks he's trash, now he's a glamor boy!"

"He's a hero, boss," Robbie replied.

"Don't give me that line again, Robbie!" Jameson shouted. "I don't trust heroes. They're nothing but criminals in disguise."

Robbie shook his head and smiled. There simply was no arguing with Jameson, especially about Spider-Man.

"Where's Parker?" Jameson asked gruffly.

"He just left," Robbie explained. "He went to cover the hostage story."

"Sure!" Jameson cried. "Another hostage story. But where was he when the Green Goblin busted through my window? We had the Green Goblin and Spider-Man right in front of our noses. A golden opportunity, and where's my photographer—out to lunch!"

143

A young editor walked into Jameson's office carrying a pair of pants.

"What's that?" Jameson demanded.

"Peter Parker's pants, sir," the young man replied. "They were in the closet, along with his shirt, tie, shoes, and socks."

"Who does he think he is, Tarzan?" Jameson shouted. "What is he doing, running around the town naked? And who put flowers on my desk?"

"I did, sir," replied Jameson's secretary, Betty Brant, from the next office. "It's your birthday. Happy birthday, sir."

"What are you looking for, Betty, a raise?" Jameson grumbled. "I don't want flowers, I want Peter Parker. And I don't want his pants, I want his photos. I want to sell papers! *I want Spider-Man!*"